STANDING IN DOORWAYS

A friend once asked me, "What's more pointless than junk email?" Ignoring the rhetorical nature of the question, I answered, "Title pages. At least spam doesn't take up space in the physical world. I can't imagine that a reader ever lived who skipped over reading the title on the front cover of a new book in favor of reading it in smaller print on the title page. It's the absolute acme or redundancy. A generation's worth of toilet paper could be saved if we tore out the TPs of all the books ever printed and used them as actual TP, though I suppose that might result in a lot of aggrieved asses."

I don't think my friend heard my little tirade as he was busy deleting emails from his phone.

So dear reader, here is the title once more in the unlikely event that you've forgotten it already after turning only a couple of pages, in which case I respectfully submit that reading may not be the best pastime for you.

Standing in Doorways

A novel
by

WES PAYTON

Adelaide Books
New York/Lisbon
2018

STANDING IN DOORWAYS
A novel
By Wes Payton

Copyright © by Wes Payton
Cover design © 2018 Adelaide Books

Published by Adelaide Books, New York / Lisbon
adelaidebooks.org

Editor-in-Chief
Stevan V. Nikolic

For any information, please address Adelaide Books
at info@adelaidebooks.org
or write to:
Adelaide Books
244 Fifth Ave. Suite D27
New York, NY, 10001

ISBN-13: 978-1-949180-38-1
ISBN-10: 1-949180-38-7

Printed in the United States of America

For the people who continually block my entry to the kitchen

by standing in the doorways of our house.

CONTENTS

PART ONE: STUDY HOUSE

Chapter One

All those assigned to Study House, which wasn't named for what was required of its residents but rather what was done to them, were in attendance—mandatory merriment. It was the spring semester mixer to welcome students back to campus after their winter breaks. This event always occasioned much anxiety for her, as she was never quite sure what was expected of the attendees, despite her having suffered through this function thrice before. She felt uncomfortable around people she had previously seen regularly but then had not seen for some time, as all the thoughts she'd cataloged about them over the course of their relationships came flooding back at once. Even if she had a mundane, nod-in-the-hallway type of rapport with the person she was now newly reacquainted, the cumulative force of the memory deluge was overwhelming. As she'd come to learn, others did not experience this same torrential sensation, though she hadn't any idea what sensations they did experience, except that they must've been felicitous in nature. The residents mingling about were invariably excited when they saw someone they knew, embracing one another and exchanging enthusiastic salutations, as if discovering after a protracted and grisly war that a close friend had survived combat, rather than just two floor mates who occasionally ate together in the cafeteria encountering one another again after a few weeks apart spent working at a mall or watching gameshows.

"You need a better second face," he said, approaching with a cup full of punch in each hand.

"You need a better opening line," she said, accepting the punch he offered.

"I'm gay, so…no, I'm good. What do you suppose they're all thinking?" he asked, gesturing with his now empty hand at the assorted clusters of students.

"I haven't any idea…it's part of my pathology. I can't read expressions or understand body language. I'm barely human."

"So you're a literal?"

"I was for a long time until I finally figured out that people rarely mean what they say. Now I don't really believe anything I'm told, which can be an advantage in college, but from what my counselor tells me is somewhat discouraged in the real world."

"What do you care? You'll have a degree from the third-best university in the country. When you don't believe what people say, they'll just assume you're being perceptive and seeing through their bullshit."

"Maybe," she said, "unless I encounter an alum of the first- or second-best university."

"You're one of the fortunate few who gets a seat at the front table. Don't be a poor sport by complaining about not sitting at the head of it."

"Good point, so what's your malady?"

"An excess of empathy," he answered. "My condition enables me to read people too accurately for comfort."

"Then you're like the opposite of me?"

"In this one, particular way…but I suspect you and I are more similar than different. I saw you standing here looking confused, while trying to put on a relaxed face, which as I mentioned needs work, and so I thought I'd introduce myself."

"I don't believe you."

"So you've told me."

"Show me something," she said. "That's Poopy over there sitting next to the vending machine. It's his senior year too. For as long as I've known him, he's kept a journal of his bowel movements, though I've never understood why."

"He's been studied for too long—"

"We all have...that's why we were given our scholarships, so that we can continue to be studied in this great social experiment known as higher education."

"Perhaps, though I'm new here, so I'm not enough of a cynic yet to agree with you completely. I believe we're also here to fulfill the school's goal of inclusion."

"Don't give me that university of diversity line."

"May I return to my disquisition?" he asked.

"Please do."

"He's been studied for too long, and it's made him feel less than...like a lowly lab rat. So to substantiate his...oh, let's call it personhood...he examines what he thinks is the product of his ugliness in hopes of seeing something beautiful and thus finding his self-worth."

"Do you think he'll ever find it?"

"Not if he keeps looking for it in the wrong place."

"What about the guy over by the punchbowl talking to that girl."

"Easy, he's schizophrenic; he hears voices in his head. They must be screaming at him right now."

"What makes you think that?" she asked.

"He has the look of someone having several conversations at once. He's trying to agree with everything the girl is saying, while telling all the internal voices to shut up or they'll ruin this for them."

"How do you know he's agreeing with her?"

"Because she's pretty."

"Tell me about her then, before she decides whether to put a dollop of hummus or a slice of cheese on that water cracker."

"Hmm…I'm afraid you've stumped me," he said. "For some reason I can't get a read on that one at all."

"It's not you, it's her…she has a constantly changing personality."

"Like the Schiz?"

"No, she doesn't have multiple personalities trapped inside of her, instead her personality continually reinvents itself, as if her mind is perpetually flipping through the channels of an internal television and she just imitates whatever show is on at the moment. Once I heard her speaking with a perfect Swedish accent…but only the one time. There doesn't seem to be any pattern at all to poor Patty."

"Intriguing…I've never met one of those before."

"And you'll never meet who she is at any given moment again…by the time she's finished eating her hors d'oeuvres she'll be somebody different…or, I guess, someone different since her body won't change. What about the handsome guy who just came in?"

"Yes, he is a cutie," he agreed, "but please stay away from him."

"Why, do you want him for yourself?"

"No, he's a psychopath."

"I've spoken to him a few times," she said. "He seemed nice enough."

"Look at his face. His mouth doesn't match his eyes."

"He's smiling."

"Exactly," he said. "It's a practiced smile that's meant to invite introductions, but his eyes are minatory…they have a saurian cruelty about them. He's a reptile hiding among small mammals."

"Thanks for the warning."

"No problem. So who's the older, thick-necked fellow in the tweed jacket that just came in from the stairwell—a kinesiology professor?"

"You really are new here," she replied. "That's one of the two horsemen."

"Who are the horsemen? And aren't there supposed to be four horsemen?"

"The horsemen are the security detail for Study House's most famous resident—the Prodigy. He only has two horsemen at a time on campus, but when we he's out in the public eye at a gala or whatever there's usually four of them. When one horseman shows up here at the dorm, you know the Prodigy will be arriving soon and that the second horseman will be hovering close by."

"What floor is he on?"

"He has several rooms, and they keep moving him around so that no one ever knows for sure which he's in."

"I can't get my own room, but the Prodigy gets several," he said. "That hardly seems fair."

"Beat him at Scrabble and maybe they'll let you sleep in one of the rooms he's not occupying."

"Right, I've read about his little project. What is it that they have him doing…studying the dictionary?"

"No, they study him while he edits the dictionary…his un-babel project, deleting useless words and rewriting definitions so that our language makes more sense."

"What's the point of that?" he asked. "It's not like this Prodigy can actually alter our language."

"I wouldn't be so sure. He's been at it since he learned to read at the age of two. They say his IQ would increase by three points every time he finished reading the dictionary from beginning to end, but that was before he came here—now he's completely untestable. He's the subject of a lifelong experiment that studies the limits of human intelligence and mental endurance."

"Why doesn't he read something else?" he asked. "From what I understand, there's a pretty decent library on campus."

"Why would he read books that contain some of the words when he can read the one book that contains all of the words?"

"I think the way the words are arranged also has significance."

"Not for him," she said. "There are those who believe that he personifies the end of original thought…that no one born after him will ever be able to think of something he hasn't thought of before, but then there are those here that know him who think he's our best chance of keeping us all from becoming just a placeholder generation. Some believe that when he's finished editing the dictionary it will be half as long and our language will be twice as precise; others conjecture that he'll distill our entire vocabulary down to just a few hundred words and that verb tenses will be rendered obsolete, enabling anyone to easily learn his new, simpler English. Imagine how different the world would be if we all spoke the same language."

"That's preposterous—one person can't change our language through editing. It has to be an organic process in which we all participate."

"Maybe," she replied. "I don't know. Either way he makes me sad…both for him and for us. But let's resume our amusing game. Let me see…okay, how about the guy near the window?"

"He farts in his sleep—a lot…and snores loudly."

"How can you possibly know that through empathy?"

"You can't," he answered. "That's my roommate."

"Why'd you choose him for your roommate if he's such a smelly, noisy sleeper?"

"I didn't. A scholarship opened up at the end of last semester. It seems during finals one of the residents here didn't feel like waiting for the elevator, so she defenestrated herself instead."

"Yes," she confirmed. "Messy business that…they had to replace the section of the sidewalk where she landed because they weren't able to scrub out the blood, so now instead of that part of concrete looking darker than the others it looks lighter."

"That's terrible."

"Not for her roommate…I heard the administration gave her an automatic pass for all her classes for last term—and she never had to take a single final exam."

"I suppose it worked out for me too," he replied with guilt in his voice. "They reopened the scholarship and gave preference to children of alumni who live in state, so I'm a midyear transfer, which seems strange to say since it's the beginning of a new year, but then higher learning lends itself to oxymorons."

"I believe the plural of oxymoron is oxymora."

"I'll have to remember that. Wouldn't it be funny if the plural was oxenmoron?"

"I'm not sure," she answered.

"Anyway, my father went to school here way back when on a boxing scholarship, and it was his dying wish for me to attend his alma mater, or it would be if he'd have the decency to just die already from the disease destroying his brain. He believes this university can make a man out me like it did him… or some such nonsense."

"You know, you talk a lot."

"Is that a problem?"

"Not at all," she answered. "I hardly ever have anything to say. So what disease does your dad have?"

"I find the parallels between the beginning of adulthood and the end of adulthood remarkable…see there, I just remarked on it. When we start out what we want is to get into a decent college, when we finish up what we want is to die a decent death. Hang on, I'm going to try out my old man voice, but I warn you, it's pretty awful. 'I'm hoping to get into the University of Aneurysm in My Sleep, my safety school is Massive Coronary State, just so long as I don't end up at Alzheimer's Tech.' As for my father, he was accepted to the Dementia Pugilistica Institute."

"I thought the voice was good, but your dad's disease sounds made up."

"It does, doesn't it? But it isn't. I wrote my application essay on how Kirk Cobain's recent suicide helped me come to terms with my father's terminal illness and how I worked through my grief by listening to Nirvana's *Ten* album on repeat for a whole day."

"Fascinating," she said. "By the way *Ten* is a Pearl Jam album."

"Is it? I didn't know that. Luckily it seems neither did the Dean of Admissions. I'm pleased to be a student here now, but the only hitch has been that the one open bed in Study House that hasn't been memorialized is with Prince Tooter over there, and I can't get any sleep. Speaking of open, someone really ought to crack that window near him."

"You know, there's a spare bed in my room."

"Oh," he said with a sly grin, "you mean you're a senior, and all seniors are assigned their own room, despite the fact that all rooms in this residence hall are double occupancy…I didn't know that either."

"See, I can tell that you're lying."

"That's just your condition talking. So are you offering me your spare bed?"

"I almost always feel alone," she said, "even when I'm surrounded by people, so the prospect of actually being alone in my own room for another semester is somewhat unsettling."

"I thought perhaps you felt that way."

"You could tell all that by looking at me?"

"Not all of it," he answered. "I requested to switch rooms, but the residence hall director explained that my only option would be to talk one of the seniors into sharing their room. I asked around and your name came up, which by the way happens to be the same as mine, though they're spelled differently, and so, as I mentioned, I thought I'd introduce myself."

"Sounds like kismet to me. You can have my extra bed on one condition. If you're getting rid of a tooter then I want to gain a tutor."

"I don't follow."

"Sorry," she said. "I was trying to do that wordplay thing you did with Tudor/Tooter. I want you to tutor me in reading people the way you do."

"Yikes, tooter/tutor—that's dreadful."

"I don't see how it's so different from what you did."

"For one thing, I did it first. For another, I did it with a crafty élan whereas you clumsily shoehorned—"

"Okay, okay," she interrupted. "I need help reading people, not with my sense of humor."

"Lesson one: it's all related. Understanding what people find funny will help you understand how they think."

"Interesting," she said. "I'll remember that."

"Sure, but don't go taking it to heart. I knew your compass was pointed in the right direction when you told me that you don't believe anything anybody tells you."

"That sounds awfully cynical for someone who says he's not a cynic."

"It's not cynicism…more like pragmatism. I learned to read people after I discovered that they rarely mean what they say."

"Maybe you and I really are more similar than different."

Chapter Two

The first week of the spring semester always felt like an end-less litany of check-in meetings with her administrators—all and sundry—to which she was assigned, each of whom con-ducted their one-on-ones with a breezy and informal tone that was contradicted by their incessant clipboard ticking and over-the-spectacles staring. She told her residence hall director that her room was satisfactory and that he need not be con-cerned about the trepidations she had expressed before the winter break to her counselor about living on her own for another semester, as her anxiety about the matter had abated, which was not technically a lie. She told her counselor that she felt somewhat, though not overly, betrayed by the relaying of her trepidations to the residence hall director, to which the counselor explained in excruciating detail the university's policy regarding counselors interceding on behalf of Study House residents when concern was warranted. She told her dean that despite her mediocre GPA and checkered academic career at the university, which she was at pains to communicate that she took great pride in attending, she didn't see the need for her to complete a senior thesis, which were widely regarded as remedial projects assigned to underachieving students whose undistinguished undergraduate portfolios were in need of bolstering. She in turn was told, in no uncertain terms, that she needed to check in with her new thesis advisor.

She knocked timorously on the frosted windowpane set in the door of office A24 in the basement of the English Building.

"Come in," instructed a curt voice from within.

She didn't like this. Extra work for her senior year had not been part of her plan. She had accrued just enough credit hours in the last seven semesters that she could graduate at the end of her eighth with the minimum number of total credits while taking the minimum number of courses to maintain her fulltime-student status, a dubious achievement to be sure but nonetheless one of which she was quite proud.

She turned the knob and timidly pushed open the door to the small, dank office. *What is it with old men and baseball? she thought as she quickly surveyed the book cases. Your childhood is gone, and it's not coming back—get over it already.* The office shelves were festooned with autographed balls, framed ticket stubs, and yellowing scorecards...all where books should've been.

"I see you're admiring my collection of souvenirs and memorabilia," said the hoary professor, sitting behind an unvarnished desk that was partially covered by an unfolded, MLB season schedule, which doubled as a blotter.

"It's really something," she replied.

"I think it transforms this humdrum office into a humdinger."

"Are you speaking Latin?" she asked diffidently.

The professor chuckled and motioned to the empty chair in front of his desk. "Have a seat. I take it you're the senior thesis writer who's been assigned to me."

"Yeah, I don't really know why," she said as she sat down.

"Let's start with a question other than 'why.'"

"Okay, how long does it have to be?"

"Or 'how.' Let's start by asking what."

"Sure…what do you think I should write about?"

"I get the sense that you haven't given this matter much thought," the professor observed.

"When? I just found out today that I had to write a senior thesis."

"I see, let's think about who then."

"Who what?"

The professor chuckled. "This conversation puts me in mind of that old 'Who's on First?' routine."

"Does it?" she asked blankly.

"Do you know Abbott and Costello?"

"Were they first basemen?"

"Never mind that now," the professor said. "So usually these theses are written about a person that the author admires. Do you have any thoughts of who you might like to write about?"

"Maybe Abbott and Costello," she answered. "They sound interesting."

"Why don't you choose someone you know a little more about? I should mention that the thesis committee tends to judge theses written about alumni more favorably."

"I remember when I was a freshman that there was a sophomore who ate fifty chicken fingers on a dare in the dining hall."

"While that sounds like quite an accomplishment, it hardly merits admiration."

"Have you tried a cafeteria chicken finger?" she asked. "They taste like dried seaweed battered in sawdust…poor kid had to go to the campus hospital."

"Be that as it may, I think you'd do well to spend a bit more time thinking of someone you would enjoy writing about for fifty or so pages."

"Fifty pages? I don't think I've written that many pages in all my papers combined since I've been here."

"And the reason why you were assigned a senior thesis still remains a mystery?" the professor asked sardonically. "Let's meet again this time next week to discuss who you've chosen… try to pick someone well known but not too well known."

"I don't understand what you mean."

"Think Alan Burgess—not Anthony Burgess."

"Were they baseball players too?"

"No dear…think George Washington Carver—not George Washington."

"Peanuts—not one dollar bill…got it."

Chapter Three

She pressed the button for the elevator in her residence hall. She knew she should walk up the three flights of stairs to her floor, but she was exhausted from all the plodding and prodding meetings she had been to as well as the prospect of now writing a thesis, so she wanted to be in her room as soon as possible in order to do nothing and to not be bothered while she did it. Besides, no one else was waiting in the lobby. The elevator arrived with a ding and the doors opened. She stepped inside and was about to press the button for her floor when three cute, cliquey juniors rounded the lobby corner and signaled for her to hold the elevator.

"Thanks," said one of the juniors, as the trio entered.

"Sure," she replied, taking two steps back to give them room.

"We only live on the fifth floor," said another junior, pressing the button for their floor. "We should be taking the stairs for exercise, but it's Friday, and I'm so done with walking."

"What floor did you want?" the third junior asked. "You didn't press a button."

"Top floor, please."

"Do you, like, have a little brother that goes here or something?" asked the button pusher.

"Why?"

"That's the only reason I could think of for visiting the freshman boys' floor," sniggered another.

"You lived here at Study House last year, didn't you?" asked the third.

"Yes."

"So you're, like, a sophomore this year?"

"No, a senior."

"You must be so ready to get out of here then."

"I suppose."

The elevator doors opened and the three girls giggled in unison as they got out.

"Enjoy your trip to the burn unit," one of the juniors said over her shoulder as the doors closed.

She could hear them laughing as the elevator continued its ascent. She pressed the button for the sixth floor so that she could get off, but she wasn't fast enough and the button stayed lit as the elevator continued upwards to seven. She was about to press the eighth floor button, but then curiosity got the best of her, so she rode the elevator to the top floor. The doors opened with a ding. Instantly her sense of smell was assaulted by a fetid, burnt plastic odor poorly masked by copious amounts of musky body spray.

"Whoa," uttered a skinny, slack-jawed freshman, sitting on a beanbag chair and playing a videogame inside his open dorm room. "There's a girl on our floor!"

Suddenly eager heads of freshmen poked out of doorways up and down the hallway like overexcited prairie dogs.

"Can we help you?" inquired a gangly teenager, stepping out of his room and tucking a spent book of matches into his shirt pocket.

"What is that smell?" she asked.

"Sorry...just a little experiment of ours," the teenager answered, with a mix of pride and embarrassment. "We're attempting to discover which smells worse: burning fake novelty vomit or burning real vomit."

"There's no winner in that contest," she said.

"Can I offer you a drink?" asked another lanky teenager, sidling up to her with a red cup in his hand.

"What's in it?" she asked.

"Just Hi-C from the cafeteria…and three pumps. But that's a pretty lightweight ratio, so I can add more to it if you like."

"Pumps…you mean like flavorings?"

"No, pumps of hand sanitizer. It doesn't really have a flavor…or at least not a good one. We drink it for the ethyl alcohol—kills brain cells as well as germs."

"How very inventive," she replied.

"I'm pretty smart," said the freshman, pointing to his neck.

"Isn't that stuff harmful if swallowed?" she asked.

"If that were true, I think they'd put it on the label."

"That's like the first warning dumb ass," said another freshman who smacked the mixologist on the back of the head.

She noticed more of them in the hallway now, and they seemed to be multiplying at an alarming rate.

"Listen, I think I got off on the wrong floor, so I'm going to go," she said, backing up towards the elevator.

"What floor were you looking for?" asked another boy unexpectedly standing behind her.

"Not this one," she said as she stabbed repeatedly at the elevator call button. To her dismay, the elevator had returned to the ground floor.

"I think I'll take the stairs instead," she announced, turning the corner and entering the stairwell. Her soft-soled shoes pounded against the hard concrete stairs; their metal, anti-slip nosing jabbing at the arches of her feet with each quick step. Invitations from the freshmen exhorting her to return echoed down after her.

By the time she reached her floor, she felt positively dizzy from her hurried, corkscrew descent. She opened the door to her dorm room breathless and frazzled.

"What's with you?" he asked, lounging barefoot on his bed and reading a magazine. "You look even more out of sorts than usual."

"Did you know there are freshmen on the top floor?"

"In a university residence hall…outrageous."

"No, I mean the whole floor is all freshman boys."

"Sure, everybody knows that."

"I didn't," she said as she sat down on her bed.

"I've only been here a week, and I figured that out. How have you been here three years and not realized that they assign all the freshman boys to the top floor?"

"I haven't any idea…don't tease me now," she implored as she took off her shoes. "I've had a rough day."

"Didn't it seem odd to you that there were no freshman boys on your floor during your freshman year?"

"Well, there were boys…I didn't ask if they were freshmen or not."

"You can always tell."

"Maybe you can," she accused as she removed her socks. "You probably think of them as re-freshmen-t."

"That's a good one," he said as he halfheartedly clapped his right hand against the folded magazine in his left. "But no…nobody likes freshman boys. They're always doing something asinine…usually involving fire and alcohol, which presumably is why they're all assigned to the top floor—if they should start a conflagration at least the rest of us will have a chance to escape. Anyway, how did your meeting go?"

"Which one?"

"The one with your dean."

"Horribly," she said. "She's making me write a senior thesis. I was assigned an advisor who's really old and really into baseball. We had loads to talk about."

"Then write about Babe Ruth—easy pass."

"Who's she?"

"That's funny."

"Is it?" she asked. "I tried playing dumb with him, thinking he might take pity on me and let me off the hook somehow, but instead I only managed to confirm for him why I need remediation."

"That's tough…trying to trade in your dignity to get out of doing something odious only to find out that your dignity isn't worth all that much."

"Yes, well it seemed like a sound enough strategy until you phrased it as such. It's so unfair…a letter of acceptance from this university is enough to impress almost anyone, but if I flunk out because of my senior thesis then I'll look like an idiot to everyone. This school is such a joke; it has this illustrious academic reputation, but hardly anyone ever goes to class. They scam smart kids into coming here by telling them, 'Step right up, this is where all the other smart kids came before you and look how well they're doing now!' Meanwhile, they're telling everybody else, 'See how clever these kids are that we're graduating!' Yeah…no thanks to you…they came in that way. Maybe it's better that we never go to class—that way there's fewer opportunities for this school to make us stupider."

"While I enjoyed the way you incarnated the university as a carnival barker, I'm afraid you're spiraling."

"And not for the first time today," she agreed. "I mean isn't higher learning supposed to involve clarity and transparency? It seems so arbitrary that I have to write a senior thesis because

I didn't meet some capricious expectations that I didn't even know were expected of me."

"Yes, the perils of a privileged education."

"It's all because of Frank," she declared as she flexed her toes.

"How's that?" he asked, lowering his magazine.

"Oh, last semester I took this Architecture Appreciation class. I thought it'd be an easy A. I mean who doesn't like looking at buildings?"

"Sure, but…"

"But our grade was split between a midterm paper and a final exam. I wrote my paper on Frank Lloyd Wright."

"Are you an admirer of his?"

"I guess," she answered. "I mean I grew up a few blocks from where he had his studio, so it's not like I had much of a choice. Anyway, I aced the paper with almost no effort—"

"Such is your modus operandi."

"And decided to skip the final since I hadn't done any of the readings all semester."

"That a girl."

"And the self-important professor tried to flunk me."

"The nerve."

"An A and an F does not average out to an F."

"Far from it, I should think."

"I protested my grade, and some secretive faculty committee raised it to a D, though it should've been a C."

"At the very least."

"Nevertheless," she continued. "I passed the class and fulfilled my last gen-ed requirement, but the professor was livid that the grade he gave me was overridden, and I'll bet he was the one who recommended that I be assigned a senior thesis."

"Perhaps, but then why not let the problem become the solution?"

"What do you mean?" she asked.

"You aced the paper on the architect, right? A senior thesis is usually written about a person, right? So then write about Wright, right?"

"That makes perfect sense."

"As it should," he said with smug satisfaction. "I solve problems. I'm the problem solver."

"I'm so hungry I can taste the remnants of my last meal in my saliva, but my feet are killing me, and the thought of walking to the cafeteria is agonizing. Would you mind giving me a foot massage, problem solver?"

"Yes, very much," he answered as he returned to his reading.

"Some good you are," she said as she started rubbing her feet. "If I wanted a man who ignored my needs, I'd get a real boyfriend."

"Then I recommend a return trip to the top floor: notions, combustibles, testosterone…all at bargain-basement prices."

The phone atop the mini-fridge between their desks rang.

"Would you get that?" she asked.

"You're full of demands today," he said, rising to his feet with the speed of baking bread and walking to the phone with the urgency of molasses. Finally on the sixth ring he answered, "Hello there."

He listened for a moment and then replied, "I don't think I'll be able to make it tomorrow."

He listened again. "Sure, next Saturday should be fine. I'll see you then," he said and hung up the phone.

"Who was that?"

"You're an inquisitive one. It was my new dentist. I'd made an appointment when I found out I was transferring, but with everything going on right now I don't think I can handle having my teeth cleaned this weekend."

"You have plans this weekend?"

"No," he answered, looking confused by her question.

She stood and picked up her shoes, walked to the window, and placed them on the sill. She slid open the heavy window.

"Don't do that," he said.

"Why not?" she asked, just as the thick stench of marijuana smoke entered through the window screen.

"Because the Psycho below us is smoking again," he answered. "I don't know when Bob Marley's birthday is, but I'm reasonably certain it's not every damn day."

"Sorry," she said, sliding the window closed with a thud.

"It's okay. His cacophonic, so-called music will begin soon anyway."

As if on cue, they suddenly heard the thundering of drums and bass guitars pulsing through the floor.

"I don't understand why he smokes marijuana to calm his nerves only to then blast that teeth-rattling, hate rock," she shouted over the din.

"Because he enjoys it," he shouted back. "Actually, I kind of like this one too. I believe it's entitled 'Change is a Process'."

"Let's process out of here and go eat dinner."

"Okay."

She put on flip flops and he slip-on sandals. The two exited their noisy room, humming the song from below as they made their way to the elevator.

"Change is a process. First you get your gun…then you kill, kill, kill!"

Chapter Four

They had made their way through the gauntlet of the cafeteria line—her tray containing a slimy Salisbury steak and a bowl of soggy cereal, his a glass of milk and a salad—but of the 64 square tables in the dining area, not a single was unoccupied. They walked slowly along the outer row of eight tables, looking for anyone who seemed as if they might soon be leaving. She espied the trio of juniors she had seen on the elevator getting up from a table near the refuse bins and the tray clearing trolley.

"I see one over there," she said anxiously.

"It's too far away. The couple that was in front of us in line is closer now."

"But if we hustle we can get there before them."

"You sound like you're actually in a hurry to eat this food."

"My meat mush doesn't exactly improve as it gets colder."

"I can't imagine it tasting any worse than it looks now," he said. "I don't want to sit next to where everyone buses their trays."

"Then what do you suggest—that we stand here like idiots?"

"I suggest that we remain calm and wait for this corner table near us to open."

"That girl just sat down."

"Yes, but she's by herself and the fellow walking over from that table of boys is working up the nerve to ask if he can sit with her."

"So?" she asked.

"So, he's not her type. She'll say she was about to join the table of girls two rows over that she hesitantly approached before she chose to sit by herself. She'll have a reason to sit with them now; they can commiserate about unwanted advances. He'll return his table of buddies, and they'll commiserate about the agony of defeat."

"How do you know he's not her type?"

"You want to wager that foot massage on it?" he asked.

"What do you get if you're right?"

"Your promise never to ask me again to give you a foot massage."

"Done."

The young man warily approached the young woman's table, waiting nervously for her to acknowledge him as he stood like a soldier at attention. She sensed he was hovering, but she didn't look up from her plate of peas and mashed potatoes.

"Excuse me…is this seat taken?"

"They're all yours," the young woman said, pretending to be pleasantly startled as she lifted her gaze. "I was about to join some friends of mine that I didn't notice until just now, so you can have the whole table."

"Well…I meant…"

"Enjoy your meal," the young woman said with a smile as she stood with her tray and left.

"Thanks."

The scene played out just as he had predicted. The young woman sat down at the table of girls, and they all shared a knowing laugh. The young man returned to the table of boys, as one saluted him and another patted him on the back.

"Voilà, the table is ours," he said in triumph, pulling out a chair for her and then taking one for himself.

"I'm impressed."

"How could you not be?"

"That was amazing…" she said, choosing not to answer his self-aggrandizing question. "The way you saw that situation setting up and knowing that she wouldn't be interested. No wonder they gave you a scholarship."

"It's all about perception and perspective."

"I get the perspective part…I don't understand it yet, but I get it," she said, breaking apart the squidgy steak with her fork. "But what do you mean by perception?"

"I don't want to sound like Yoda—"

"Who's he…a social philosopher?"

"In a manner of speaking," he answered. "Are you really not familiar with *The Empire Strikes Back*?"

"I think I was in kindergarten when that movie came out, so it was a little before my time."

"A timeless film can't be before your time."

"I don't really like movies anyway—too much dialogue."

"You're ridiculous," he said, stabbing at his lettuce. "Anyway, I'm beginning to think that you don't pay attention to people because you get overwhelmed by them—all their talking and such—so you've conditioned yourself to ignore them…as a kind of coping mechanism."

"That's interesting, but what does it have to do with perception?"

"I think that rather than ignoring them, you ought to perceive them differently."

"How so?" she asked.

"Don't see them as people—with the confusing things they say and their body language that must seem like so much meaningless movement—at least not until you feel comfortable around them."

"I don't know if that'll ever happen."

"Baby steps. Start by seeing people as something else… maybe as tokens, like pieces on a game board. Strip away the things about them that don't make sense and just pay attention to the parts of them that do. Once you feel comfortable with that perception of them, then start to focus on the parts that you don't understand—but only one part at a time. I think this is what we all do anyhow, but most of us have a built-in autofocus, though I suspect yours is broken. However, maybe you can turn that problem into a solution by exercising your ability to adjust your aperture manually. Perhaps in time you'll train yourself to see people better than the rest of us can."

"An example please."

"Let's see…there's the Schiz leaving the cafeteria line and looking for a table. Watch as he moves around the dining hall."

"He's walking straight along the far column of tables," she observed.

"Just like a rook in chess."

"So what's that supposed to tell me?"

"It doesn't have to tell you anything yet," he answered. "At this point it's merely information that's easily understood—just file it away."

"Alright, here comes pattern-less Patty with her tray," she said. "True to form, she appears to be walking aimlessly through the tables."

"Her seemingly irregular route belies a pattern of sorts."

"She walked two tables to her right and then one table to her left. Now she's walking one table to her right…and two tables to her left."

"Despite her apparently erratic path," he said, "you can predict where she'll end up within a reasonable margin of error, even if you don't quite know how she'll get there."

"Okay, I see it now…Patty is a knight."

"Yes indeed, and here comes Poopy—let's watch what he does."

"He sees the Schiz and Patty sitting down together at the opposite corner of the grid, so he's going to…walk diagonally through the middle of all the tables and join them. He's a bishop."

"And something of an interloper."

"I think it's nice when crazy people find each other," she said. "So I don't need to do anything with what we saw…just remember it?"

"Right, those details are puzzle pieces. Collect enough of them and they'll start to fit together to reveal a larger, more complete image."

"Now we know who the knight, bishop, and castle are, but who's the king?" she asked.

"You are, since you're the observer," he answered. "Without you there would be no game."

"I thought the Prodigy would be the king."

"No, he's the thimble," he said, looking around. "As far as I can tell, he's playing a different game completely…you know, I've never laid eyes on him down here, or anywhere else for that matter"

"I think they must bring his food up to him."

Chapter Five

It was a sunny Sunday, as all Sundays should be, and exceedingly temperate for late January. The campus was in the midst of one of those rare Midwestern winter warm spells that are as short-lived as they are infrequent. They had taken portable food from the cafeteria—her a grilled cheese sandwich made by stuffing three slices of cheese between two slices of bread into a single slot of a toaster, resulting in an unsurprisingly goopy mess, him an apple and a handful of croutons—to watch the pickup games of Wiffle Ball that were played on the lacrosse field behind Study House when the team wasn't practicing. They spread a shower curtain liner from a dorm bathroom on the ground, which was still wet from the premature thaw, far behind home plate that itself was a repurposed plate from the cafeteria. She chewed, he crunched, and they both sat and watched the young men take their turns swinging the silly, yellow bat.

"Instead of Waffle Ball, they should call it Whiff Ball for as much as they strikeout," she said, expecting a guffaw, or at least a chuckle, for her droll observation.

"What do you mean?" he asked, failing to pick up on any humor in her remark.

"You know 'whiff' instead of 'waffle'…because of how often they miss hitting the ball."

"I know what you mean by 'whiff'… but do you think this game is called Waffle Ball?"

"Isn't it?" she asked.

"No, it's called Wiffle Ball."

"I thought it was called Waffle Ball because the ball has holes in it…like how waffles have holes in them."

"Waffles don't have holes," he said. "Holes go through an object…like a hole in a sock. Waffles have cavities."

"That's interesting, because I've never played golf before, but I'm pretty sure if I made a hole in one the golf ball wouldn't come out in China."

"You make a good point," he admitted.

"Do I? Because it occurs to me now that French fries with holes in them aren't called waffle fries…oh, wait they are."

"Yes…another good point—you're on a hole roll," he said, "but this game is called Wiffle Ball for precisely the reason you had previously mentioned. The combination of the slender bat and the ball with perforations that cause it to move through the air unpredictably results in many strikeouts or 'whiffs.'"

"It must be so marvelous to know everything."

"Clearly I don't, but if I did, it wouldn't be. Frankly, I'm rather impressed by how you filled in your lacuna of knowledge about this absurd game derived from baseball. After all, your explanation of Waffle Ball makes as much sense as Wiffle Ball, which isn't even spelled the same way as 'whiff.' Besides, in the right light, the color of the batter's bat even looks a little like waffle batter."

"Thank you…although it'd make me feel even better if I knew what the word 'lacuna' meant."

"It means 'cavity' or 'hole'…or maybe I just made it up," he said, offering her a crouton. "Did you know that a Wiffle is a unit of measurement used in marine biology?"

"Of course not," she answered, taking the crouton.

"Wiffle balls are a good size and shape for measuring sea coral, and the holes keep them from being flattened by the pressure of deep water."

"That's ludicrous."

"Maybe so, but that doesn't stop it from being true. Did you also know that the state of New York once declared that Wiffle Ball was as dangerous a recreational activity as scuba diving?"

"Now you're just showing off."

"Yes," he agreed, "but I hope you'll indulge me, as I'm afforded so few opportunities to do so."

"How do you know all that? Did your dad invent Wiffle Ball or something?"

"No, I briefly dated an oceanography major. My father called him Maritime Mary…and once, at a Memorial Day barbecue, Marine Mary, which is what passes for wit in my little town."

"You're from a small town, huh?" she asked with a curiosity she seldom felt for anyone.

"Yep."

"It must've been tough growing up there. I'm surprised you didn't get away sooner."

"It can be difficult to leave your hometown…in ways that are both good and bad."

"So your dad…what's he do?"

"He's a police officer, or rather was until his diagnosis. My father enjoyed punishing wickedness as he likes to call it, but not for the sake of justice I think. Like a hunter who laments the extinction of his quarry, he would've been sad if ever there were no longer any wickedness in the world."

"So he boxed when he went to school here?"

"Yes, he was a bantam. He held a school record for most consecutive wins, which he still takes great pride in, even though the university disbanded the program soon after he graduated."

"What's a bantam?"

"In boxing, a weight class of about a 120 pounds. In people, a small and combative person…which is also apt."

"I'd sort of pictured him as a big man."

"His small stature belies the vast disappointment contained within."

"You know, a lot of stuff belies other stuff with you."

"Is that right?" he asked rhetorically. "So tell me about your parents?"

"They were nice enough…did the best they could. It's hard to love a child who doesn't love you back. When I was twelve my mother told me that she'd had a son years before I was born, but that she'd given him up for adoption just after he was born. She used to say that I was her punishment for not having loved him enough."

"Do you see them often?"

"Not since I came here."

"It's barely been a week since the term started."

"No, I mean when I came here my freshman year." She smoothed out a crinkled patch of plastic under her knees.

"Oh…then what do you do over the summers?"

"Usually work on campus and sublet an apartment, though I spent the summer after my sophomore year working on a cruise ship…that was horrible."

"What about winter breaks?"

"You're technically supposed to leave the dorm, but all the staff is on vacation, so I just hang around. It's not like they check every single room before they go."

"But don't they lock the lobby doors?"

"Of course," she answered.

"Then when you go out how do you get back in the building?"

"I don't go out...I hang around inside the building."

"What...what do you do for food?" He took the first bite of his apple and then wiped away the juice that had sprayed on his chin.

"I keep some things in the fridge and save up nonperishables from the cafeteria...maybe buy some noodles at the store. You know you can make pasta in the microwave, right?"

"But why would you want to...I mean, why would you want to do any of that? Doesn't it get lonely? Don't you get bored?"

"Don't you get lonely and bored when you're at home?"

"I suppose," he answered. "I spend most of my time in my room reading or watching TV."

"Same with me."

"But it must be eerily quiet."

"I don't know about 'eerily'...I find it perfectly, peacefully quiet."

"There's something that puzzles me."

"I'm pleased to have puzzled you."

"The reason you let me share your room is because you didn't want to be alone," he said, "and yet you prefer to spend your vacations rattling around the deserted dorm as if you were a ghost."

"That's exactly what I'm afraid of," she said grimly. "I always prefer to be alone. If I had my druthers I'd be invisible. The winter vacations for me are a break from the noisy, never-ending interactions with people that I hardly ever understand. I hate when that break comes to an end like all vacations must, but as with any good vacation, afterwards I feel rested and renewed, ready to deal with my everyday reality again. For me, the first couple months of last semester in my own room were heaven, but then I started to feel myself getting used to the solitude...the vacation had turned into my new normal, and I feared I was growing so unaccustomed to being around people that I'd become even more ill at ease in their company…like a prisoner who becomes institutionalized after being held for too long in solitary confinement."

"That's fascinating," he said. "I completely misread the reason you wanted a roommate."

"I hope you're not disappointed."

"On the contrary. I'm delighted to be wrong about you. So what are your plans for spring break?"

"The same," she answered, "haunting an empty residence hall."

"No, let's do something together over spring break… maybe you could come home with me for a visit."

"Sure, maybe…that sounds nice. Look, our downstairs neighbor is up to bat," she said, taking a renewed interest in the game.

"He has such droopy eyelids. I can't tell if he's sleepy or high or about to murder someone."

"I think his eyes look smoldering and smoky."

"So would that make his right eye smoldering and his left smoky?"

"Hush," she ordered, "I want to watch him bat."

"Do my words block your vision?"

"Oh no…strike one."

"It's probably hard for him to see the ball with his eyes mostly closed."

"Why don't you like him?"

"I need a reason to dislike a known psychopath?" he asked.

"It's just the way he's wired. He hasn't done anything to anybody."

"I don't have a problem with the Psycho. I have a problem with you being attracted to him."

"Darn, strike two…you know, you sound a little jealous."

"I'm not jealous—I'm concerned," he said. "He's the only boy I've ever heard you express any interest in, and he happens to be a hate-filled predator masquerading as a college student."

"He has more love inside of him than I do...at least he loves himself," she said nonchalantly. "I imagine I'm more like him than anybody else in Study House."

"Don't say that."

"I won't say it if it bothers you, but that doesn't mean it isn't true. I don't want to kill anyone, but I also don't understand why it's verboten. Most people only take up space and use up resources. He thinks the world would be better off if there were fewer people on it...I mean come on, he's not wrong. Look—he got a hit."

"No, it's a fly ball. The centerfielder is probably going to catch it...yep—he's out."

Dejected, the batter dropped his bat and skulked away from home plate, but suddenly his attention was aroused when the centerfielder called out to him, "Hey Psycho, you really killed that one—too bad you missed the gap. Let's hope your aim is as off when you finally decide to climb the clock tower."

The batter stopped midstride, pulled a small notebook from the pocket of his baggy sweatpants, stared for a moment at the centerfielder, and then jotted something down with a stubby pencil.

"What's he doing?" she asked.

"Uh oh, it appears that the centerfielder just made the Psycho's enemies list."

"How do you know that's what's in his notebook?"

"Because he has a sociopath's superiority complex, and he perceives anyone who challenges him as a threat that needs to be dealt with before they can damage his inflated self-image. Haven't you ever noticed the way he talks down to people that intimidate him?"

"I thought he talked like that to everyone."

"Maybe he's more insecure than I realized. Regardless of the degree, his psychosis is as obvious as it is tedious."

"You sound like one of my doctors," she said.

"I think all of us in Study House have spent enough of our lives being psychoanalyzed that we should each be awarded an honorary psychology degree."

Chapter Six

She was back in the basement of the English Building, knocking on the door of office A24. It had been a week since she'd spoken to her thesis advisor, and she felt just as uninspired as she had before their last meeting.

"Come in dear," said the professor.

"How did you know it was me?" she asked, as she entered his office and sat down.

"Aside from the fact that we have an appointment...I could tell it was you by your forlorn knock. Reminds me of an old cartoon of a doleful frog knocking on the door to a Biology 101 classroom."

"Then what happened?" she asked.

"I presume the frog was invited in to be dissected."

"The cartoon didn't show the dissection, did it?"

"No...no, just the frog knocking on the door."

"That doesn't seem like much of a cartoon," she said. "Was it a half-hour long?"

"I think we're talking about different types of cartoons."

"I'm glad to hear it," she said, feigning relief. "That hardly sounds appropriate for children."

"I believe that the innocence of youth is safe in this instance. So, have you thought any more about who you'd like to write your thesis on?"

"I have," she began. "I want you to know that I've given the matter a great deal of consideration. I even skipped all my classes since we last met in order to really think the matter through."

"I wish you hadn't done that; moreover, I wish you hadn't told me that."

"I think it was a smart decision, because you're really going to be impressed with the person I've chosen."

"Well...I'm an old man. Don't keep me in suspense, dear."

"One Mister Frank Lloyd Wright."

"Wrong."

"What do you mean Wright is 'wrong'?"

"A previous professor of yours, who shall remain nameless—"

"I know his name," she said crossly, folding her arms.

"—made a point of mentioning at a faculty social function, this tedious biannual affair, that you had previously written a superb paper on Frank Lloyd Wright for his class, and went on to suggest that you should use this thesis as an opportunity to...how did he phrase it exactly...'expand your breadth of knowledge so that you might soar high, stretch your analytical muscles so that you might roam far' by writing about someone else. I grant you, his statement strains under the burden of the mixed metaphor, unless he was comparing you to a griffin, in which case the statement is gratuitously grandiose, but nevertheless I agree with his sentiment."

"Phooey," she cursed.

"Now, now—there's no need for imprecations. You told me that you spent the last week thinking of someone to write about; surely you must've considered other possibilities. After all, people are like ballparks...some are more appealing than others, but all are interesting in their own way."

"What about the inventor of Wiffle Ball?" she offered, as she scanned the professor's collection of pennants hanging on the wall behind him.

"Who?"

"I don't know who…and that's the real travesty," she declared. "We've all heard of Wiffle Ball, but no one knows anything about its origins. For far too long there's been a shameful lacuna in our culture's knowledge about such an important form of recreation derived from our national pastime."

"As much as I appreciate your conviction and your use of the word 'lacuna'—I don't think that choice would merit the academic rigor of a senior thesis."

"Double phooey."

"Don't despair—you'll think of someone. Do a little research…peruse some scholarly journals."

"That sounds about as boring as listening to baseball on the radio."

"I know you're discouraged and so didn't mean that, but if libraries aren't your cup of tea then dial up the World Wide Web that all the hebetudinous youngsters seem so enamored with for fact finding these days. I'm sure the resources it has to offer are as reliable as any other."

"Now that you mention it, I did recently do some research on a student athlete who attended college here some years ago. He was a bantam weight boxer, and he holds the school record for the most consecutive wins."

"That sounds promising," the professor said. "What's his name? What year did he graduate?"

"Oh, I don't quite recall…but—"

"I see…why don't you take the weekend and come back on Monday morning prepared to tell me more about this alumnus."

"I'm not sure the weekend will be enough time to do the sort of exhaustive research my potential thesis subject deserves."

"It feels to me like we've got a man on first with a sizeable lead and a woolgathering pitcher. Better to steal second sooner than wait to be batted in later."

"I don't follow," she said.

"Comeback in three days not seven."

Chapter Seven

She entered their dorm room ready to give Mister Let-The-Problem-Become-The-Solution the business about his useless advice, but he was not there. A note on their telephone read: If the dentist calls, please reschedule my appointment for next Saturday.

She sat on the bed, removed her shoes, and looked out the window. It had been a dreary day, and now, just as the sky was growing dark, it began to rain. At least she had made it back without getting wet. The raindrops blotched the window screen on the other side of the glass. She watched as the water clogged the pores of the metal mesh. The phone rang. She put on her flip flops and left the empty room.

She walked down the hall to Poopy's room. She entered without knocking. Poopy was sitting at his desk, writing with deliberation in his journal. "Hey Poopy, do you want to have dinner with me in the cafeteria?"

He looked up from his desk, surprised that she was standing in his doorway. "I'm a senior now...I'd prefer if you didn't call me Poopy anymore."

"I'm going to continue calling you Poopy for as long as you keep writing in that poop diary of yours."

"This is important information, and please don't say 'diary'—it sounds too much like diarrhea."

"Well poop log sounds too much like what comes out of you."

"On a good day. Today I struggled to poop three tiny turds. They each looked like russet swans. Do you want to know what I named them?"

"Of course not," she answered. "I want to go eat some food. Think of it as fodder for your next journal entry."

"We've both lived in this dorm going on four years now, and we've never once had dinner together. Why do you want to eat with me now? "

"Because suddenly I find you fascinating."

"I don't believe you, but I'd be glad to be your dinner companion. However, you should know that the Schiz will be joining us."

"Ugh, I hate watching that guy eat. It always looks like he's trying to masticate and talk to himself at the same time."

"He doesn't do that anymore," Poopy said. "Hasn't since sophomore year."

"Is that so—then let's go."

The threesome exited the cafeteria line together. She let the two boys take the lead to see which chess pattern they would follow to find a table, but as they approached the first row the corner table became available, and so the trio sat down.

"The head table," Poopy remarked. "This is our last semester, and I feel like we're the three kings of the cafeteria."

"A triumvirate," the Schiz said aloud. "A troika," the Schiz said to himself.

"More like three stooges who should have better dinner plans for a Friday night," she said. "Besides the king's table would be near the middle of the row."

"You'll miss this place once you're gone," Poopy replied.

"Will I?" she asked. "Remember, I don't have a sense of nostalgia."

"You may not have a sense of nostalgia," Poopy countered, "but you have a sense of smell. I imagine you'll think back on this dining hall fondly whenever you catch scent of overcooked meats being served by under-washed cafeteria workers."

"I believe taste may be the most nostalgic sense to remind us of our youth," the Schiz said aloud. "People smell different as they get older," the Schiz said to himself, "and of course they look different, sound different, and feel different...but I bet they taste the same."

"Once I leave here, I don't want to smell or taste anything from this cafeteria ever again."

"Never say 'Never,'" Poopy cautioned her.

"I didn't," she corrected. "I said 'ever.'"

"Remember Kimmy who graduated our freshman year?" Poopy asked.

"Kimmy the klepto," the Schiz said aloud. "The stealer of hearts," the Schiz said to himself.

"Sure," she said, "the actress."

"Kimmy couldn't wait to leave here and move to Los Angeles," Poopy said. "Now she comes back to campus every year for theater week."

"That's because she has nothing better to do," she said. "She comes here to reminisce about playing Ophelia and Blanche DuBois. What's she going to brag about out there? Her one callback for a Dr. Pepper commercial?"

"Have some charity for poor Kimmy," Poopy said. "It's hard being an aspiring actress."

"Aspiring actresses actually have an easier time of it than their male counterparts," she said. "Since hardly any actresses are cast in their first role beyond their twenties, they can be reasonably sure by their third decade that if they haven't been cast in something yet then they probably never will be and can go on to have a career in another field. It's men, however, and their potential to be cast in their first role well into middle age, that have the greater potential to waste their lives chasing dreams of the silver screen."

"Astute observation," Poopy said as he noshed on a flaccid onion ring. "I'd wager though that even if she did meet with some success, she'd still return to campus for the adulation. I figure members of her cohort out there are likely better consolers than congratulators."

"Maybe so," she said, turning her attention to the Schiz who seemed to be drifting from the conversation. "You look tired. I seriously doubt you found a girlfriend, so you must be staying up late to study."

"They just moved the Prodigy to my floor last night. The horsemen are noisy and never sleep," the Schiz said aloud. "And they never let anybody use the restroom when his highness is on the throne," the Schiz said to himself.

"I don't think he's stayed on my floor since early last semester," she said. "I guess that means I'm lucky."

"Not so lucky in everything. I heard you were assigned a senior thesis," the Schiz said aloud. "I'm sure that'll go well," the Schiz said to himself. "They say they're easier to write when the author chooses a subject who has a similar disposition, so if she picks an apathetic misanthrope, it should practically write itself."

"Yeah, I'm pretty bummed about it." She made swirls in her insipid tartar sauce with the rubbery nub of a fish stick. "I haven't chosen anyone to write about yet. Did either of you guys get assigned one?"

"Nope," the Schiz said aloud. "I actually went to class and did my homework," the Schiz said to himself.

"I wasn't assigned a thesis," Poopy said. "But I'm going to write one anyway on Thomas Crapper. Many people errone-ously think he invented the toilet, but in reality—"

"Stop," she interrupted.

"That'll really complement your polisci degree," the Schiz said aloud with sarcasm. "I actually wanted to hear more about Thomas Crapper," the Schiz said to himself.

"We're trying to eat here," she said.

"I'll never understand why the egress of food is an un-acceptable topic of conversation during the ingress of food."

"Because it's not food when it comes out of you," she said.

"Manure is the best fertilizer," Poopy said defensively. "It nourishes the farmer's crops, which grows into the food we eat. Should we not discuss agriculture during meal times either?"

"The thought of it is unpleasant," the Schiz said aloud. "Al-though, I do rather enjoy a solid evacuation in the morning," the Schiz said to himself.

"Is it so much more unpleasant than what's on our trays now?" Poopy asked. "I bet my average bowel movement smells better than the fried bologna sandwiches the cafeteria served for lunch today."

"If you're about to extend an invitation for us to make a comparison," she said, "I'd ask that you retract that invite into the dark recesses of your colon."

"I think part of why we find the topic so repellent is that it's a completion of a human cycle, which we're hardwired to have an aversion to, because it reminds us of the end of the larger human cycle that awaits us all," the Schiz said aloud. "Though I see more obituaries in the newspaper than birth announcements, so maybe that theory is crap," the Schiz said to himself.

"But it makes no sense," Poopy said. "Every synonym for 'food' is acceptable, but the word 'poop' is considered puerile, the word 'excrement' explicit, and the word 'shit' vulgar. It's not fair."

"It's not fair to what...feces?" she asked.

"Yes," said an exasperated Poopy. "It's an important bodily function that deserves some reverence."

"Then perhaps we ought to say 'bless you' when somebody farts," she said facetiously.

"Maybe have a moment of silence when someone flushes a toilet," the Schiz said aloud. "This is a pretty crappy conversation" the Schiz said to himself. "Yes, it's going down the tubes rather quickly." "I disagree, this is more interesting than the usual shit we talk about." "Potty mouth."

"You two are just full of it," Poopy said.

Chapter Eight

She hadn't slept much. She'd spent most of the night listening for sounds in the hallway. The various conversations of her floor mates died down around midnight. After that there were the occasional pairs of footsteps accompanied by tittering whispers and the periodic flushing of toilets from the floor's restrooms, but the night had passed without her hearing the sound she was waiting for—a key in her door lock.

She lay with her eyes open, staring up as the morning sun revealed cracks in the ceiling tiles. Did he leave campus? Had he found a boyfriend? Was he hurt? She strained to understand why she cared so much, but she couldn't find the answer anywhere in her head. She had detested her last three roommates, though sharing a dorm room with them had been good practice, and in time she'd learned to tolerate their habits and cope with their idiosyncrasies, but if any of them had suddenly disappeared while they had lived together, she would have considered the quiet and calm that resulted from their absence a windfall. Now the quiet of the room caused her to wish that the Psycho below would blast his obnoxious music, and the calm caused her insides to chafe at the abrasive rub of being alone.

She lifted herself out of bed, put on her flip flops, and walked to her desk. She rummaged around in the drawers until she located the campus directory. When she found the number she was looking for, she removed her roommate's note from the phone's keypad and dialed.

As the phone rang, she ruminated over the word "dial."

"Hello," a groggy voice answered.

"Is this bulimic Becky?" she asked.

"No one calls me that anymore," Becky said sternly. "Who is this?"

"It's me...your roommate from sophomore year."

"I still live with my sophomore year roommate. We moved out of that madhouse two years ago. You're that insane girl I lived with my freshman year, aren't you?"

"I guess it was freshman year...time flies," she said. "Who was my sophomore year roommate then?"

"I have no idea. Listen, it's stupid early for a Saturday. What do you want?"

"I...uh...want to know how you're doing."

"No you don't."

"No, I guess don't," she said and knew it was true.

"Is there anything else?"

"Do you know why we still call it dialing a phone, even though they all have keypads nowadays?"

"Don't call me again," Becky enjoined.

The line went dead. She listened to the dial tone for a moment, imagining that it was the sound of a trauma patient's flat-lining electrocardiogram. The noise was soothing to her. She returned the handset to the cradle and began to dress for breakfast. She hoped the cafeteria was serving pancakes that she could slather in butter and drown in syrup.

Chapter Nine

Aside from going downstairs to the cafeteria for an early breakfast and then a late lunch, she had spent the whole of Saturday
alone in her room. By noon on Sunday she thought it a good
idea to go outside, not so much for the fresh air, but more so
that when her roommate finally did return and asked what she
did over weekend, she could truthfully answer that she had
gone out. She could lie, of course, and stay in her room but tell
him that she had been out, but he would know it wasn't true.
Somehow he just would, she thought.

She went to the lacrosse field to watch the Wiffle Ball
games. Though still unseasonably warm for the time of year,
this Sunday was cooler and less sunny than the last, so there
were fewer boys playing. She espied pattern-less Patty sitting on
a crazy quilt far afield near the parking lot. She walked toward
Patty, twice waving when Patty had looked up from her book,
but each time Patty only looked down again, evincing neither
recognition nor acknowledgement. In way of salutation as she
neared Patty's positon, she said, "That's quite a motley quilt."

"My grandmother made it for me just after I was born,"
Patty said, picking a blade of grass and closing it in the gutter
of the book to mark her spot. "She started with a disappearing
nine-patch design, and then altered the pattern each time my

crying changed. She knew about me years before the doctors ever agreed on a diagnosis."

"Do you mind if I sit down?"

"Not at all," Patty answered, "but please sit facing me rather than sitting next to me. It's easier for me to hear you that way."

"Sure, okay." She sat on the opposite edge of the quilt with her feet in the center near Patty's. "So what are you reading?"

"Huxley's *The Doors of Perception*," Patty answered. "It's usually what I read on Sundays."

"You must really like it."

"Sometimes."

"I hope you don't mind my asking, but I've always been curious...what exactly is your diagnosis? I've never quite understood...you."

"That's a succinct if not subtle way of putting it. The me I am now appreciates your candor. Most people either dance around my condition or ignore it all together. I suffer from acute decision fatigue, and my personality changes are a coping mechanism that psychologists find fascinating and are heretofore completely incapable of curing."

"I get it," she said. "It's like the sound of your voice. For most people it evolves naturally and they never consider how they arrived at it, but for me if I keep to myself for several days—as is my wont—it atrophies from disuse. Then when I finally do need to speak, I first have to remember what I'm supposed to sound like. Half the time, I don't even know if I'm pulling it off or if I sound completely different than I did the week before, but oddly I always recognize recordings of my voice while others, who settled into their natural voice years ago, often say they sound like strangers to themselves."

"That's because they never think of how they sound until they're confronted with a recording. Their voice evolves internally just as it does externally as they age, but usually not in the same way. So when they speak they may hear a voice in their forties that's more resonant and fuller of confidence than it was in their twenties, but what others hear might in fact sound shriller and more strained."

"So then the way I have to decide on my voice is the way you have to decide on everything?"

"Yes," Patty answered. "I don't unconsciously prioritize and automatically make the thousands of tiny decisions throughout the day the way everyone else does. Some doctors have speculated that if not for my continually-changing personality, I would either deliberate over every decision as if it were life or death and never get out of bed, or I would treat each decision as arbitrary and one day capriciously walk into traffic."

"Your psych's are right—that is fascinating," she said. "If you learned to control your changing personalities, couldn't you exhibit almost anyone's voice and mannerisms?"

"Yes," Patty answered with a sigh. "I'm sure I'd make a really excellent ventriloquist…a job I've always never wanted."

"Then you'd have to learn to operate a dummy. You'd be better off as just an impressionist."

"But I don't know how to paint," Patty said with a wry smile.

"That's funny," she said with a stone face, recognizing the bon mot rather than reacting to it.

"Then why didn't you laugh?"

"It's not in my nature," she answered, "though lately I've gotten better at identifying humor."

"That sounds like progress."

"I suppose," she said. "So we've lived in the same building for four years now, and I hardly know anything about you. What are your plans after you graduate?"

"Oh plans...I don't make plans," Patty answered blithely. "I'm simply going to go somewhere, do something, and hope for the best."

"That doesn't seem so different from what I had in mind."

"I'd like to do something that brings joy to people, like work at a doughnut shop or a barbecue restaurant. Maybe work Christmases at the mall as one of Santa's elves."

"I don't think the alumni newsletter is going to be in any hurry to spotlight your career choices."

"I don't care about that sort of thing," Patty said. "College has been like a four-year sleepaway camp for me. I'm not in a rush for these prelapsarian days to end. The one common thread of my ever-changing personality is that I never fear the future. Imagine how insufferable I'd be if each new personality dreaded choosing a career or was anxious about achieving the expectations of adulthood."

"I watched my parents suffer all manner of hardships and indignities in their careers, trying to grasp at advancements that were forever just out of reach."

"I find myself continually revising what my definition of an adult is in order to ensure that I'm not becoming one," said Patty, "but one thing I'm certain of is that contentment has only one level. If you're content with what you have, then no good can come from chasing what you don't."

"Not letting the exceptional become the enemy of the acceptable," she paraphrased. "That seems like a wise way to live."

"I can tell you're apprehensive about the future," said Patty, "but never despair of the possibility that everything will work out fine."

"You really think it can?" she asked, intending for the question to sound rhetorical even though it wasn't.

"I've never been more certain of anything," Patty answered.

"This is the longest conversation we've ever had. I wish I hadn't waited until our senior year to get to know you better."

Before Patty could respond a gust of wind caused the corners of the quilt to flutter. As the two smoothed out the quilt and used their outstretched hands to weigh down the corners, a Wiffle ball rolled between them.

"Sorry ladies," called out a young man, advancing toward them from his position in right field. "The breeze carried that one farther than I thought it would."

"Stop—you stay there." Patty picked up the ball as she stood up and deftly threw it to the young man.

"Nice throw," the young man said as he caught the ball. "You're welcome to join our game."

"Not interested" said Patty, sitting down beside her quilt mate rather than across from her as she had been. "Sorry, what were we talking about?"

"Uh…life after college," she said as she shifted toward the edge of the quilt so that her shoulder wasn't touching Patty's.

"Oh, that drivel about me working at a donut shop or a BBQ joint."

"Don't forget about being one of Santa's elves."

"I'd never do that," Patty said. "I loathe x-mas."

"So then what do you think you would like to do?" she asked.

"Maybe go to grad school," Patty answered. "I could see myself as a professor, and summers off wouldn't be the worst thing. Besides, I don't think I'm ready for the postlapsarian days after college."

"What would you teach?"

"Who cares? Surely not the dunderheads that would only occasionally attend my lectures."

"Wouldn't the publish-or-perish atmosphere of academia be sort of a drag?"

"Competition is a human conceit," Patty said. "It both hinders and helps us."

"Do you think the Prodigy will become a professor too?"

"Digy, a professor...I doubt it."

"I've never heard him called Digy before," she said.

"It was my pet name for him...we had sort of a spring fling last year."

"I didn't know that," she said with astonishment. "I always imagined that he was asexual."

"I'm sure his handlers would prefer that," Patty said, "but no...we had a fervid albeit fleeting affair."

"That's fascinating—I knew there were rumors that you got around, but I had no idea you and...Digy—"

"I'm pleased I could be such a source of fascination for you," Patty said, twisting her face into a moue.

"Sorry...I didn't say I believed the rumors."

"People talk. What can I do about it? Besides, I can't help it if ever boy I meet is interesting at first and then suddenly they aren't. Anyway, the me I am now still appreciates your candor."

"Do you think you and Digy will ever get back together?"

"There's no edification in the second sting of the scorpion."

"I've heard that sentiment expressed differently before, but I like your version better," she complimented. "So if not a professor, then what?"

"He'll manifest his genius by doing something completely familiar yet totally unexpected."

"Such as...?"

"I don't know," Patty answered, "but the enormity of its impact will result in a lacuna so abysmal that the rush to fill it will feel like a black hole to all those around him."

"I love your use of the word 'lacuna,' but that sounds ominous," she said. "Are you sure?"

"I've never been more certain of anything."

Chapter Ten

"Where have you been?" she demanded as she sat up in bed, wearing her nightshirt and sleeping shorts.

"You'll make a really excellent divorcee someday," he said as he entered their dorm room. He dropped a travel bag on his bed and then plopped down beside it.

"I was worried about you."

"I left a note," he said, kicking off his shoes.

"About the dentist."

"Well, I wouldn't have left a note about the dentist if I'd been abducted or was going off to kill myself."

"So I should be thankful that I didn't find a ransom or suicide note instead?"

"Remember to get the house in the divorce—that's how you know you've really won."

"By the way, the dentist's office never called."

"Yes they did," he said. "You just didn't answer the phone, but I called them from home to make sure they moved my appointment."

"Maybe I was out," she said faintly. "So you went home?"

"We should get an answering machine."

"I agree," she said. "A machine that gives answers would be preferable to a roommate who doesn't."

"Why are you in such a snit?" he asked. "I thought you'd be glad to see me."

"If you thought I'd be glad to see you, then you should've known that I'd be sad that you left without letting me know where or why you'd gone."

"I'm sorry," he said. "It was inconsiderate of me. Why don't we go downstairs and have dinner? I'm famished."

"The cafeteria closes early on Sunday nights," she said. "I waited as long as I could for you, and then got in right before they shut the doors."

"That was nice of you to wait."

"They had tater tots."

"Those are my favorites."

"I know," she said as she switched off their room's overhead light.

"Hey, I just got home," he protested. "I'm not even in my pajamas yet."

"Sleep in your clothes. I have to be on campus in the morning."

"You don't go to Monday morning classes," he said, switching on his desk lamp.

"You don't know what I do. For your information, I went out this weekend too."

"Where...to watch the boys play Wiffle Ball?"

"No, I had a nice chat with Patty."

"And where did you two have this chat...the cafeteria?"

"No," she answered, "we went out."

"Like to the lacrosse field?"

"We were closer to the parking lot."

"Well that's quite a change of pace," he said sarcastically.

"Shut up...so you went home?"

"Yeah, my father's health has deteriorated again. His condition seems to worsen every winter, and apparently this year's bill just came due."

"I'm sorry."

"Thanks," he said. "I think it's just a matter of time now."

"That's true for all of us."

"Yes," he said, "but he's got less of it than most of us."

"I didn't realize your father was in such a bad way."

"He actually seemed to be in good spirits, all things considered, and was lucid for a few long stretches over the past couple of days. He asked to come visit me and see how the campus has changed."

"That's great," she said. "I'd like to meet him."

"Why do you want to meet my father?"

"Because I think I'm going to write my senior thesis about him."

"That's peculiar," he said as he changed into his sleepwear in the half lit room.

"Is it?" she asked. "I think writing about alumni is practically de rigueur."

"I thought you were going to write about Frank Lloyd Wright."

"I suggested that to my thesis advisor, but it seems the faculty has conspired to prevent me from recycling my old paper."

"Oh, the humanity," he said, "but still, aren't there other alumni you could write about?"

"Maybe, but all the well-known alumni have already been written about ad nauseam, and just think of the research required to find another alumnus nobody remembers."

"I see your point."

"Do you think he'd mind if I interviewed him?" she asked.

"I'm sure he'd be delighted to reminisce about his glory days…so long as he can remember them."

"Then it's settled. All I need to know now is his name."

"It's the same as mine."

"We all have the same name? That's incredible."

"It's not incredible; it's a coincidence," he said, as he switched off his desk lamp. "Your mother named you after her favorite actress, whereas my father named me after himself. If you ask me, we were named by people too self-involved to be competent parents. Now let me get some sleep."

"Why are you in such a snit?" she asked.

"I'm just tired…it's been a long weekend filled with family drama…like something out of a Tennessee Williams play."

Chapter Eleven

"Blackout!" a voice shouted from the hallway. She opened her eyes but couldn't see anything. She thought she'd just fallen asleep, but her extremities felt stiff as if she'd been sleeping for hours. She willed herself to sit up, and her body reluctantly obeyed. As she waited for her eyes to adjust, she thought about the last thing she remembered. She had been lying awake in the darkness of the dorm room, wondering why her roommate seemed upset that she had chosen to write her thesis about his father. She would've asked him, but after a few minutes of thrashing about angrily in his bed, she heard the heavy breathing sounds of his slumber.

She still couldn't see him on the other side of their small room. She hadn't drawn the curtains before she went to bed, but there was no light coming from the streetlamps or nearby buildings through their window. Had the voice she heard yelled blackout? She'd thought that had been part of a dream, but if it wasn't, why hadn't her roommate also woken up? Perhaps she was still dreaming, but asleep or not she was urgently aware that she needed to pee.

She didn't own a flashlight, which she now knew was a mistake. She thought of waking her roommate to ask if he had a flashlight, but she was fairly sure he would say that he didn't, even if he did, and would likely be cross about being woken up. She slid her toes into her flip flops, stood, and opened the door to the darkened hallway. She heard hushed voices coming from the bathroom and could see a sliver of light under the door to the women's side of the restroom. She held out her hands to feel for the hallway wall. Finding it, she followed the wall toward the restroom, nearly falling into the small alcove for the water fountain.

After another misstep at the fire extinguisher, she reached the restroom door. She opened the door slightly and peeked inside. A lit candle in a sink gave off a dim, flickering light. The whispering voices seemed to be chanting, though not quite in unison. A few of the steadier sounding voices were leading the chants and the other, less-certain voices sounded as if they were trying to follow along. Had she stumbled on a coven of witches? Maybe she was still asleep.

Abruptly the chanting stopped. She didn't know how many necromancers were in the restroom, but she could tell they were moving around now. She opened the door a little more, and in the silence the hinges creaked. She froze. The movement inside the restroom ceased. She held her breath and looked again through the door. Suddenly her view was blocked by a pair of glassy eyes staring back at her from the other side of the door.

She ran down the hallway until she was on the opposite side of the floor from her dorm room. She crouched in the darkness and waited for the sound of the restroom door's hinges, but instead the light from under the door disappeared. Now she really had to pee.

A few yards in front of her was the illuminated exit sign above the stairwell door. She moved stealthily toward the stairwell, not rising out of her crouched stance. She pushed into the stairwell and kept a hand on the door so that it would close silently behind her. The battery-powered emergency lights above the stairs illuminated most of the steps, but their eerie green glow could not penetrate the darkened recesses of the intermediate landings. As she descended the stairs, she wondered if she should squat in the corner of the half landing to do her business, but she was worried that someone might bump into her in the dark, and so she thought better of it. She pressed on, passing through the darkness of the intermediate landing and the steps below into the darkened hallway of the floor beneath hers.

Once more she followed along the hallway wall toward the restrooms, and again she heard voices, but this time they were coming from the men's side of the restroom. Unlike the whispered chanting she'd heard upstairs, she could hear these voices loud and clear. Two men were having an innocuous although animated conversation about footwear.

"I'm telling you, Dr. Martens are the best shoes for standing."

"Not better than Footjoy."

"Absolutely, better than Footjoy."

"No way, I can walk all day in my Footjoys and my feet feel fine when my shift is over."

"I didn't say walking. Footjoys are great for walking, but for just standing you can't beat Dr. Martens."

"I don't know about that. Anyway, I don't like the way they look."

"What are you, a GQ model? Besides, Footjoys look like old-man shoes."

"They're golf shoes. We play golf."

"So does my dad, and he wears Footjoys."

"Well my son wears Dr. Martens, or Docs as he calls them, and he dresses like he's in a damn grunge band."

She entered the women's restroom and fumbled in the darkness for the nearest sink. Her fingers soon found cool porcelain. All the restrooms on the residence floors had the same layout, so she felt her way past the four sinks and turned right. After a few steps, she touched the metal partition of the first toilet stall. She hastily opened the door, dropped trou, and sat down. In short order she experienced the satisfying relief of an overfull bladder being emptied.

As she was finishing, she heard the two voices from the men's room addressing a third, frantic voice.

"I'm telling you, I really need to use the bathroom."

"And I'm telling you that you can't use this one while it's occupied."

"He's just one guy. Why does he need four toilets?"

"Take it up with the residence hall director in the morning if you want, but right now you need to wait or use another facility."

"But it's dark."

"You think we don't know that?"

"Listen, I really need to go."

"You need to go all right—you need to go away."

"This is my floor, and my bathroom, and I'm going to use it."

She heard grunting noises followed by what sounded like a body being thrown through the restroom door into the hallway. The third voice was shakier now. "I'm putting you both on my list...and him too." She could hear the Psycho's stifled whimpering as he retreated down the hall.

She waited a few more moments until she was sure the episode had reached its conclusion. She tried to flush the toilet, but the lever was unresponsive. Apparently the flushing mechanism required electricity to function, which she thought strange. She pulled up her shorts and made her way to the sink, but again discovered that there was no water pressure. Maybe the height of the residence hall necessitated water pumps and the power outage had knocked them offline.

She departed the total darkness of the restroom for the nearly complete darkness of the hallway. The illuminated exit sign above the stairwell door offered scant light, but it was the only visible landmark, and she walked toward it. As she passed the men's restroom, she could hear the two voices again. The first louder than before and the second muted.

"How are we doing in there, sir?"

"Did you think he fell asleep?"

As she entered the stairwell, her feet splashed in a shallow puddle and her nose was assailed by the acrid smell of urine. A voice behind her muttered, "Don't scream."

"What?" she whispered as she turned around. Without warning, a pair of hands grabbed her neck.

"I told you not to scream."

"I didn't," she gasped.

"Where are you going?"

"Upstairs…to my room."

"Are you going to tell anyone that I peed in the stairwell?" the Psycho asked as he squeezed her neck harder.

"No," she replied. "I considered doing the same thing."

"Why?"

"Because there are witches in my bathroom," she answered.

"What?"

"Witches," she wheezed.

"Are you mocking me? I could kill you and no one would ever know who did it."

"Well, I think you might be on the shortlist of suspects, but go ahead and kill me if you want. I don't care what happens to anybody…including myself."

"You shouldn't test me," the Psycho warned. "The doctors have known since I was a child that I'm capable of murder."

"I don't think there's anything wrong with you. We need people who can cull the herd so that the Earth's human infestation problem doesn't grow out of control."

The Psycho loosened his grip slightly and pulled her to him, kissing her with his open mouth as if his kiss might become a bite. She kissed the Psycho back, using her tongue to lick his lips like a wolf cleaning a wound. The Psycho slowly moved his hands from her throat toward her chest, but she pushed him away.

"Some other time," she said as she took a step backwards.

"We could go to my room. I don't have a roommate."

"Not tonight...I like to have the lights on so that I can see who I'm with. Besides my feet smell like piss."

The Psycho leaned against the stairwell door as she ascended the stairs to her floor. She returned to her room, locked the door, kicked off her wet flip flops, and climbed into bed with her roommate.

"Hey, I'm trying to sleep here," he groggily protested.

"Then go back to sleep, but there's a blackout going on, and we need to protect each other from all the weirdos out there."

Chapter Twelve

"So why exactly did you get into bed with me last night?" he asked, laying on his side with his cheekbone resting on the heel of his hand.

She woke up, unsure of why the room looked different. She blinked hard at the morning sun coming through the window as she scanned the room to locate what had changed. The room was the same, but her perspective of it was different. She thought she had heard her roommate's voice. "Did you say something?"

"Yeah, why are you in my bed?" he asked again.

She rolled over and was startled that she was face to face with her horizontal roommate. She remembered now coming back to their room after her misadventures the night before.

"There was a blackout," she said as she scooted toward the far side of the small bed.

"And?"

"I had to pee."

"So you thought in the event that you experienced night-time incontinence it would be better if you were in my bed."

"No, I went to use the bathroom, but then there were… weird girls in there, so I went downstairs and ran afoul of the Psycho—"

"Are you okay?" he asked earnestly.

"Yes, I'm fine. In fact the incident offered a surprisingly pleasurable moment of frisson…it was just a lot to process in the middle of the night."

"So you were frightened and wanted me to protect you? I can understand that given my muscular physique," he said as he raised his free arm and flexed it. "I've been working on my triceps."

"Triceps…more like try-harder-ceps," she joshed. "I've seen mussels that are stronger."

"Hold on—I liked the first one, but then you lost me with the second."

"You know, mussels…like clams."

"I think that only works if we're at a seafood restaurant… or maybe in print, but even then—"

"So a seafood joke only works if you can see the food?" she asked.

"Now you're trying too hard."

"What if we're at the seafood restaurant, and I say: I've seen more muscle tone on a jellyfish."

"No one eats jellyfish," he said.

"I've seen more muscle tone on a jellyfish sandwich."

"Okay, I think that's enough for so early in the morning."

"Yeah, I've got to get to a meeting with my thesis advisor anyway," she said. "Are you sure you're alright with me writing about your father?"

"Why wouldn't I be?"

"That's what I'm trying to figure out. I mean I understand that you don't like him much, but why would you care that I'm writing my stupid thesis that nobody will ever read about your dumb old dad…you're supposed to be tutoring me, remember?"

"I've always thought that my dad took up boxing because he had a girl's name—thought he had something to prove… like the boy in that Johnny Cash song."

"The one written by Shel Silverstein."

"Right," he said, "but then his queer son came along and ruined the macho image he'd created for himself. I don't know…maybe it's not something that makes sense if I put it into words."

"Then doesn't that mean it just doesn't make sense at all?"

"Possibly…whether it makes sense or not you should write your thesis on whoever you want."

"Are you sure?" she asked.

"Sure I'm sure, but I don't want to talk about it anymore—okay?"

"Sure—okay."

Chapter Thirteen

At first she thought maybe she was in the wrong building; the basement was pullulating with professors and students moving to and fro. Lively, esoteric conversations could be heard in every corridor. Some offices had queues outside their doors several undergraduates long, but no one waited in front of door A24. So she knocked…feebly.

"Could I prevail on you to knock once again with more vigor?" the professor asked quietly from the other side of the door.

She knocked harder, this time on the frosted glass with the side of her fist rather than rapping the wood above the doorknob with her knuckles.

"Yes, do come in," the professor bellowed.

"What was that about?" she asked as she entered the office and closed the door behind her.

"I apologize for requesting that bit of theater, but I do appreciate you indulging my entreaty with your histrionics."

"Sure, but what was that about?" she asked again.

"You may have noticed that the bowels of the English Building are more enlivened this Monday morning than they have been the past two Friday afternoons when you visited my office."

"Yes, I practically saw a brawl breakout over whether Hamlet was written by some guy named Francis Bacon."

"Just out of curiosity, what's your opinion concerning that volatile issue?" asked the professor.

"It makes sense to me."

"How so?"

"Hamlet…piglet…Bacon," she answered tersely. "Seems elementary. Maybe he also secretly wrote the screenplay for that movie Babe."

"The one with John Goodman?"

"Which animal did he play?"

"I'm not sure dear," said the professor, rubbing his abruptly throbbing right temple in hopes of staving off a headache.

"So why is it so congested out there?"

"As you may have observed during your time at this university, some professors are rather lax about actually being in their offices during their appointed office hours." He watched as the expression on her face receded into vacancy. "Or perhaps not, but trust me, most professors—particularly the younger ones—keep hours that would make a banker blush. I'm of the old guard and think it important to be where I say I'm going to be when I say I'm going to be there, whether it's weekend-eve or not. I've endured no small amount of ribbing for immuring myself in this office for hours on end, especially when I have so few visitors these days, and so I do my best to remind my colleagues that students still come to see me occasionally."

"That sounds…bizarre."

"Yes, well I sincerely hope that you never find yourself yielding to the yoke of office politics."

"Like they say, you can't make an omelet without breaking some eggs."

"They do say that, though I'm not sure why they would in this context," the professor said, as he moved his massaging fingers to his forehead. "Anywho, have you done any further research since last we spoke?"

"I have," she answered. "I now know the name of the student boxer in question. It's the same as mine."

"That's progress then and also rather intriguing. There's something of a tradition of athletes who've had that name. In fact, when I was a lad I played ball with one—meanest short-stop I ever met."

"However, I'm not sure that he would make such a good topic for my senior thesis after all."

"Why not?" the professor asked. "From what you mentioned last time, he sounds like a promising candidate."

"Well, he also happens to be my roommate's father."

"Splendid, so many subjects of these theses are no longer with us, often resulting in papers rife with dry, secondary sources. Do you think you would be able to interview this alumnus?"

"I think I can when he comes for a visit sometime in the next few weeks, but my roommate seems upset by the idea."

"Why do you think she is bothered by the prospect—"

"No, my roommate is a boy."

"Oh, I saw in your file that you are a resident of Study House. I didn't realize that was allowed."

"It isn't technically, or at all, so don't tell anyone, but it's okay—he's gay."

"What a progressive living arrangement."

"Besides, I'm a virgin...sex isn't really my thing," she continued, "although we did sleep in the same bed last night."

"That's plenty of information, so let's get back to—"

"But I did make out with a psychopath yesterday while standing in a puddle of his pee, and it wasn't as terrible as it sounds."

"Weren't you assigned a counselor you can talk with about this sort of thing?" the professor asked as he kneaded the base of his skull.

"We don't meet until Friday. Besides, she'd just tell me something like 'I'm sublimating sex with school work,' which is absurd since I do about as little of one as the other. I think she sublimated being an inane busybody with a psychology degree. If I had to guess, I'd say my creative procrastination is really a manifestation of—"

"Perhaps you can make an emergency appointment with your counselor," the professor suggested. "Her inanity notwithstanding, it sounds as if you have some issues you should talk through posthaste, and I'm not really qualified for that sort of thing. I'm better suited to offer assistance if ever you find yourself in a quandary about Dickens."

"Eww—there's no need to be graphic. I mean really...the idea of it, slithering all over each other like two earthworms trying to breathe in wet dirt after a heavy rain, waiting to see which of you can produce the most moisture."

"Interesting imagery, but what I meant was—"

"Why don't we put my personal issues in abeyance and focus on my thesis?" she asked.

"A capital idea."

"Why would my roommate have a problem with me writing it about his dad?"

"I have no earthly idea." The professor took a long, deep breath followed by a protracted exhale befitting his level of frustration. "Have you tried asking him?"

"Yes, but he doesn't want to talk about it anymore. Aren't you supposed to be advising me on writing my thesis?"

"Let me think a moment, dear. Does your roommate possibly have a strained relationship with his father?"

"Yes, but what does that have to do with this?"

"I haven't a clue."

"Could it be that he's afraid that I'll find his dad more interesting than him? But why would he care what I think...I don't care what he thinks."

"Are you sure that's true?"

"I…don't know," she said, considering for the first time the possibility that she, in fact, did care. "What does caring feel like?"

"Sometimes it feels like an ache in your head," answered the professor. "Other times it feels like an ache in your heart."

"I don't want either of those."

"I don't blame you, but it's hardly ever a matter of choice. Why don't you take a few days to sort this out? Then come back on Friday to let me know where things stand…that is, after you've spoken with your counselor."

Chapter Fourteen

As she ascended the stairs from the stuffy confines of the English Building's basement, she recalled she had a Comparative Literature class (whatever that is) that she hadn't yet attended, which started in a few minutes on the ground floor, so she found the room, peeked inside, and noticed with agitation that one of the fluorescent bulbs in the ceiling's light fixture was flickering. She decided to try again closer to midterms. Surely maintenance would replace the bulb by then. If the professor gave her any grief, she could claim the flickering was just the sort of distraction that her counselor had urged her to avoid for mental health reasons. Being a resident of Study House had its advantages.

As she exited through the building's portico, she saw Poopy leaning against a nearby column. "You look distraught," she said as she punched him not gently on the shoulder.

"What was that for?"

"I was attempting to cheer you up."

"By hurting me?" he asked as he rubbed his shoulder.

"It was a playful hit meant to roust you from your funk."

"Playful hits don't leave a bruise."

"I'll have to work on that," she said. "Just be glad I didn't hit you on the chin. I saw that technique in a movie once, but frankly it seems a little advanced for me."

"Probably so…maybe you should avoid the punching altogether and instead simply ask what's the matter."

"I only wanted to make you happy…or at least less sad. I don't really care what the matter is."

"That's a nice thing to say." Poopy watched her glow. "That was sarcasm, by the way."

"Oh…but then why should you care if I know what your problem is? There's probably nothing I can do to help you, so you'd just be wasting both our time by telling me."

"I haven't pooped in three days."

"See," she said, "there's absolutely nothing I can do to help you with that."

"Anyway, how did you know I was distraught?" Poopy asked. "Since when do you read people?"

"I've been working on it lately."

"And the whole wanting me to feel better thing?"

"Just something I'm trying out," she answered. "Hey, have you tried eating prunes?"

"Thanks for the patently obvious advice."

"You're welcome," she said as she turned to leave.

"That was sarcasm again."

"In that case," she said over her shoulder as she walked away, "I hope your colon bursts and the festering feces infects your abdominal cavity."

"Good talking with you," Poopy chirpily called after her, "and nice alliteration." Maybe she had cheered him up some, he thought as he went off to the Comp Lit class that neither knew they shared.

The midmorning air felt warmer on her skin than it had when she'd entered the English Building, putting her in a spring state of mind. She strolled along each length of the decreasingly crowded main quad, watching as her fellow students filed into the prosaically named Natural History Building, Foreign Language Building, Chemistry Building, et al. until she was one of the last remaining amblers. As she neared the Student Union, a leafleteer tried handing her a handbill about who the hell knows what.

"No thanks," she said.

"Don't you care about reparations?" the serious young man asked as he matched her stride.

"I don't know what that is, and I have no desire to find out, so it seems I really couldn't care any less."

"If someone stole your inheritance, would you care about that?"

"Please stop keeping step with me. I was enjoying a nice walk by myself."

"I can walk where I want; it's a free country."

"Apparently not, as I'm not free from being bothered by you," she said as she quickened her pace.

"Answer one question for me, and I'll leave you alone," he beseeched, panting slightly as he accelerated to keep up.

"Fine," she said, stopping altogether and putting her hands on her hips. "What's your question?"

"Do you mind if I catch my breath first?"

"No. So will you stop pestering me now that I've answered your question?"

"Clever," the young man gasped, "but that wasn't my question."

"Then spit it out."

"Do you think it's fair that between 1789 and 1865 the United States refused to pay for over a 100 million hours of forced labor by people abducted from Africa and that it continues to deny compensation to their descendants, despite acknowledging in the Thirteenth Amendment that slavery is unlawful?"

"Of course not."

"Oh," the leafleteer replied. "Usually the other person has more to say."

"I can say a little more. Since fairness is important to you, answer a question for me."

"Okay."

"I agree that your cause is just, but do really think the federal government, which can't even fund social security, is ever going to find the money to pay what's owed to the ancestors of slaves?"

"Of course not."

"Oh," she replied. "That's not the answer I was expecting. So then why are you doing this?"

"Because I believe in it."

"That's a good answer," she said. "Now give me your pamphlet and then stop following me."

"Here you go," he said, handing her a leaflet. "Have a nice walk."

Chapter Fifteen

She'd spent the rest of the morning walking around campus, exploring places she seldom had occasion to visit during the previous three years. She circled the antiquated observatory several times, admiring its purposeful curves. She tried to count the misty panes of glass on the side of a long greenhouse. She happened upon a secluded sculpture garden in the courtyard of the Industrial Design Building.

Her newfound appreciation for the comely campus had her considering Patty's possible plan of becoming a professor, but her musings soon dissipated when she thought of her abysmal grade point average. She imagined a paper-pusher at the registrar's office rolling his eyes as he pulled her future transcript off a printer. The thought of a world with one less opportunity of which she could avail herself made her despondent, and all her walking had made her hungry. She figured she could ameliorate the pangs of both conditions by consuming a confection of some sort. A slice of cake wasn't quite what she craved. A piece of pie perhaps? No, she wanted something sweet but also a little savory. The elusive thought of a triangle-shaped pastry swirled around her head like a tiny boomerang. Then it hit her: baklava.

She headed to her favorite gyro joint, Greeker than the Greeks, on Jade Street. As she rounded the corner onto the commercial thoroughfare that bifurcated the campus, she noticed an answering machine in the storefront window of a secondhand shop. She ducked inside, the bell above the front door signaling the day's first customer.

"Can I help you?" asked an old woman with a kindly voice from behind the counter.

"Yes, does that answering machine in the window work?" she asked, approaching the counter.

"We don't sell anything that doesn't."

"How much is it?"

"Ten dollars," the woman answered.

"Would you take five?"

"I'd take two fives."

"Can I see it?"

"Of course you may." The clerk retrieved the device from the window, blowing off a bit of dust as she returned to the counter, and then presented the machine to the store's sole customer for inspection.

"It looks to be in pretty good shape," she said as she popped out the microcassette and examined it.

"If you like, I can plug it in so you can test it."

"That's not necessary," she said, as she eyed a basket of pinback buttons near the cash register. "Would you throw in one of those?"

"Sure honey, pick out whichever one you want while I ring you up."

Chapter Sixteen

She still had the pleasing taste of honey and pistachios in her mouth when she returned to their dorm room. He spun around in his desk chair as she entered.

"Girl Power?" he asked, reading the button pinned to the lapel of her jacket. "Since when?"

"What do you mean? I'm a girl aren't I?"

"Sure, but I didn't know you were a feminist."

"Women's empowerment is something I believe in, okay?"

"Yeah," he said, "of course...okay."

"I got us an answering machine," she said, pulling the corded device from a brown paper bag.

"Lovely."

"Shall we hook it up and record a message together?"

"I don't know, that's a big step in our relationship."

"We've already slept together," she said as she set the machine next to the phone, "so I don't think this is too much of a stretch."

"I'll plug it into the socket, while you hook it up to the phone."

"What should we say?"

"How about: leave a message," he said as he strained to reach the outlet between their desks.

"Let's do something more original, like I'll say 'hello' as if I'm answering the phone, and then after a long pause you say 'gotcha, we're not actually here right now.'"

"Yeah, I think that's original every time I hear it."

"Sarcasm, right?" she asked.

"Right—you're really getting good at identifying it."

"I had some practice today."

"Alright," he said as he stood up, "it's plugged in."

"Yep, it's all hooked up here."

"So what are we going to say?" he asked.

"Something memorable; it's going to be an indelible record of our voices—except that it'll be a tape…and we can erase it."

"Yes, I'm familiar with how answering machines work."

"Any ideas?" she asked.

"Nothing leaps to mind."

"Me neither."

"I think we're putting too much pressure on ourselves."

"Fine," she said, "I'll just press the record button, and we'll say whatever comes to us."

The machine beeped, prompting them to begin their recording.

"Hello," she said tentatively.

"Please leave a message," he said, making it sound more like a question.

Chapter Seventeen

It was Wednesday, which meant taco night in the cafeteria. She liked to smash several hard shells on her plate and then add a layer of shredded cheese, ground beef, diced tomatoes, and jalapeños to make a nacho platter of sorts. He preferred a tidier taco experience, filling three soft shells with equal parts chicken, sour cream, and lettuce.

They found a vacant table in the far corner. She crunched, he chewed, and they both sat and watched their fellow students traverse the dining hall, looking for either empty tables or empty chairs next to friends.

"I think it's time for another installment of 'What will Patty do next?'" he said, nodding his head in Patty's direction as she left the cafeteria line with her tray.

"Okay, Patty is scanning the tables," she observed. "Patty sees the Psycho eating by himself and cautiously moves in his general direction."

"And what will happen next?" he asked with the voice of a gameshow host.

"He'll make creepy eye contact, and she'll fake acknowledge someone else sitting far away."

They could see the Psycho lift his head, but from their vantage point they could not see his expression, though Patty's reaction was clear enough. She suddenly gave a small wave to someone behind him and walked past.

"She wasn't waving at us was she?" he asked.

"I don't think so," she answered. "She appeared to be looking at the clock on the wall behind us."

"In that case," he said in his gameshow voice again, "what will Patty do next?"

"Her head's on a swivel, she's perusing her options…I imagine she's getting overloaded with choices right about now, so I feel a personality change coming on—"

"Time is winding down," he said, sotto voce, to underscore the dramatic denouement of their little game.

"Okay, I can do this. She's…"

"Yes…"

"Wait, I've almost got it." She glanced behind her, not at the clock on the wall but rather at the entrance to the dining hall below it. "I was wrong before. She wasn't looking at the clock; she was looking at the Schiz who just came in, but—"

"But?"

"But he didn't see her," she said with excitement. "She's going to dump her tacos and then get in line behind the Schiz so that she can eat with him. She's going to let him decide where they sit."

"That's a bold prediction. Let's see how this plays out."

Patty continued walking along the center column of tables, but then hooked a sharp left when she reached the middle row, moving toward the refuse bins and clearing trolley. She dumped her tacos in the garbage and put her plate and tray into the trolley. Then she walked past the entrance. The cafeteria worker checking meal cards at the door gave her a confused look. She took her spot at the end of the line, three people behind the Schiz. He noticed her and smiled; she returned a pleased but surprised expression.

"Well done," he congratulated with mock applause.

"Thanks—it was touch and go there for a moment."

"Honestly, I would not have predicted such a startling turn of events."

"I think I've figured out what makes Patty tick," she said.

"Then the student has become the master."

"What are you two so happy about?" asked Poopy, approaching with a plateful of jalapeños, a bottle of hot sauce, and an anguished countenance. "I could stand to hear some good news right about now."

"I see the prunes didn't help," she observed.

"Not yet, so I'm trying something a bit more extreme."

Chapter Eighteen

She was scheduled to meet with her counselor and thesis advisor that afternoon, but she didn't feel she'd made any progress thinking through the situation with her roommate, or rather the more she thought about it the more complex the issue became in her mind, and she didn't want to explain it to someone else until she could articulate it for herself, so she skipped both meetings and spent most of the day walking around campus. It was the third time since her extended stroll on Monday that she'd spent the better part of her day in such a manner. Despite her aching feet and throbbing calves, she always felt better after her long walks. For part of the afternoon she'd even joined a large tour group of prospective students and their parents. She envied the experiences that lay ahead of the eager teenagers, despite knowing that not all of those experiences would be pleasant. She mused about how she might do it all differently were she to start her college career over.

She could hear her phone ringing as she arrived at the door to her dorm room. She turned the knob, but the door was locked. Her roommate must be out. She fumbled with her keys as she rushed to unlock the door, but then remembered that the machine would answer it, so she relaxed and found the correct key, likely more quickly than she would have in a panic. As she entered the room, she saw a flyer on the floor that must've been slid under her door while she was gone. She picked it up as the answering machine clicked on; the outgoing message started with her roommate's voice: "We're not in right now, so leave a message. If this is the dentist's office calling to confirm my appointment for tomorrow, please reschedule it for the same time next Saturday."

She was irritated that he'd changed their outgoing message without asking but thought it was a clever way to avoid a tedious phone call. The machine beeped, and she heard the professor's voice. "This is your thesis advisor. That must be your lodger on the machine. I missed you at our meeting today. I hope you were able to make your other appointment to discuss that matter you mentioned last time. We'll try again for next Friday, though stop by in the morning as your machine reminds me that I too have a dental exam next Friday afternoon. I dislike the dentist. We've got ducks on a pond, so let's hit them in."

Ducks on a pond...what in the world does that even mean, she wondered. Was the professor using a wildlife metaphor to elucidate a baseball analogy? Did he sound a bit inebriated? Maybe he spent Fridays alone in his office getting his own start on the weekend. She turned over the crudely photocopied flyer and read the text, which was circumscribed in a large circle:

Floor Party
This saTURDay Night!!
See you 'round, unless you're square.

She loathed parties of any kind. She could barely tolerate people when they were sober and acting normal. Get a few drinks in them with the expectation that they be entertaining and they become completely unbearable. Rather than contemplating the reason for the party, she began cogitating reasons not to attend. Perhaps she could try one of her long campus walks at night.

"Are you coming?" asked someone behind her, standing in her open doorway.

"I doubt it," she said, turning to see who the owner was of the familiar voice she couldn't quite place.

"Too bad," said the Psycho. "It should be fun."

"You got one of these?" she asked, holding up the flyer. "You don't even live on this floor."

"Someone posted it in the bathroom downstairs. It's all anyone is talking about, so I had to come up and see it for myself."

"See what?"

"Poopy's perfect circle. He saved it. It's in the first toilet of the men's room on this floor. It's actually quite impressive."

"What are you talking about?" she asked.

"I heard he hadn't pooped in over a month, and then this morning he woke up and dropped a flawless ring."

"It's been more like a week…anyway, how's that even possible?"

"The prevailing theory is that it took so long because there were two cables twisted around each other in his colon, blocking themselves in, but then when they came out together they unfurled, connected at the ends after weeks—"

"—days," she corrected.

"—days of being compacted by intestinal pressure; however, I think it was really just one long strand and the two ends joined in the round bowl of the toilet. Either way, it really is a perfect circle…you can't tell where it ends or begins. I can walk you into the men's room if you want to see it."

"Of course I don't want to see it," she snapped.

"Well, I want to see more of you, so maybe reconsider coming to the party tomorrow night."

Chapter Nineteen

"What can one say on such an august occasion?" the Schiz asked aloud of the group assembled in the floor's common area. "It's February not August," the Schiz said to himself. "If you're like me," the Schiz said aloud again, answering his own opening question, "you say a great many things but keep most of them to yourself."

The Schiz was acting as Poopy's herald, who was seated on a mock throne-toilet, gilded with aluminum foil and an intricate filigree of colorful bubblegum that had been chewed and stretched into strands. Atop his head rested a crown made from empty rolls of toilet paper. He held a plunger in his hand as a scepter and wore a sash of tp. He was drunk as a lord and had the look of a Rodin figure in repose.

"Tonight this Potentate of the Potty..." the Schiz declared aloud, "this Aristocrat of the Anus..." the Schiz declared to himself. "...has deigned to grace this court's humble shitdig with his noble presence; he who has recently laid waste, or rather laid a waste specimen of such flawless geometry that it remains on display in our fair restroom."

Several people clapped with enthusiasm. One anonymous voice shouted, "It stinks—get rid of it."

"Anticipating your plaint, good sir, it has been decreed that our liege's log can only be dispatched by a royal flush, but our Sovereign of Scat has decided…" announced the Schiz aloud, "Our Sheik of Shit has chosen…" announced the Schiz to himself. "…to burn his journal chronicling the last ten years of his excremental exploits, as no more perfect poop will ever be expelled by any living thing that sits or squats upon this earth than that which was shat by his majesty, the Sultan of Splat."

This final pronouncement was met with uproarious applause. Someone from the back whistled loudly.

"Hear ye, hear ye!" the Schiz proclaimed aloud, attempting to both calm the small crowd down and work them up. "Hear me too," the Schiz proclaimed to himself. "Fellow floor denizens, a few firebug freshmen have offered to oversee the journal's funeral pyre, and against our better judgement we're going to allow them."

Three eager teenage boys standing near a pair of trashcans, one partially filled with crumpled paper the other completely filled with water, saluted with lighters in hand.

"First it's only fitting for our King of Crapping to say a few words, and so I give you the Patron Saint of Poop…" the Schiz intoned aloud. "His Ass-Holey-ness…" the Schiz intoned to himself. "…the Despot of the Deuce, the Doyen of Dung, the Duke of Defecation…the inimitable Poopy."

Poopy slowly stood from his stately throne, steadying himself against the toilet's faux tank lid. He waved regally to those gathered around him. He started to speak, then stopped, and then started again.

"Oftentimes life can seem like a long, endless turd with an undefined start and an indefinite finish," Poopy slurred and then burped. "Other times it can seem like nothing at all, and you feel as if you're trying to poop someone else's shit. However, I know this much my friends: if you stay the course and never, ever give up—eventually…everything will come out in the end."

His audience considered the sage words carefully for a moment, and then simultaneously and spontaneously erupted into a unanimous cheer. Poopy raised his scepter in victory, smiling for the crowd, but then his expression turned to one of distress. He unceremoniously dropped his scepter and scurried to the half-empty trashcan, puking in it as well as on the shoes of a nearby freshman.

After a few seconds, Poopy lifted his head and addressed his subjects once more, "But sometimes it comes out the other way."

His audience cheered heartily again.

"Do you think they'll still burn Poopy's journal?" she asked, sipping a plastic cup half full of nondescript beer.

"I overheard someone at the keg saying that the Schiz was going to clean Poopy up and maybe try to sober him up a little too so that he'd remember at least some of the lighting ceremony," he answered.

"That's thoughtful…and ridiculous."

"How they're going to make a mini-bonfire without setting off the smoke detectors is anyone's guess."

"The freshmen disabled them," said the Psycho, who was suddenly standing next to them. "From what I understand, these tamper-proof detectors require more than merely taking out the batteries, but apparently, through a lot of practice, they have perfected the technique."

"Oh, hello," she said.

"A good evening to you," the Psycho said as he made a crisp bow. "You look ravaging tonight."

"The word is 'ravishing'…genius," he said, rolling his eyes.

"Some men are men of words, some men are men of action, and some men aren't men at all," the Psycho said with a scowl.

"And some men should be locked away," he said, matching the Psycho's glare. "Aren't you going to write my name in your cute little enemies list now...like the child who can't make friends that you are?"

"I didn't bring it with me, but I promise that your name will be added before the night is out."

"Be sure to write it correctly so there's no confusion; I know spelling can be tricky for you philistines."

"I'll put a note next to it: guy with girl's name who isn't a man."

"Okay boys," she said and took a long drink. "I'm thirsty, can one of you gallant gentlemen get me another drink?"

"Sure," he said, taking his roommate's cup. "I could use another myself."

"Try not to spill any queer...I mean beer," said the Psycho.

"Good one numb nuts," he said as he walked away.

"I thought we'd never get rid of him," said the Psycho.

"I wasn't trying to get rid of him," she said. "I was trying to keep the peace. You should be nicer."

"Nice really isn't my thing."

"Could not behaving like an ass be your thing?"

"Lots of luck with that," said Patty as she approached the couple. "I'm looking for Digy. I heard he's here with some slut from Date House. Have either of you seen him?"

"I've never heard a harlot call another woman a slut before," said the Psycho.

"Who says 'harlot' anymore?" asked Patty. "You make me sound like a character from the Bible."

"I wouldn't be surprised if one day God turns you into a pillar of salt," said the Psycho.

"Oh you're just grumpy because the only time you ever have sex is when you're by yourself," said Patty.

"Do the girls of Date House really go out with whoever the university assigns them to?" she asked.

"They don't have to," answered Patty derisively. "Just like the boys of Football House don't have to play football."

"What is that you all are talking about?" Digy asked, approaching with an attractive coed in tow. "Lambskin or pigskin?"

"The pig part is right," Patty said, turning up her nose.

"Since when are you at liberty to attend floor parties?" asked the Psycho. "I thought they kept you under armed guard with your head buried in the dictionary."

"I get a night off from time to time for special occasions."

"And this qualifies?" she asked in disbelief.

"The triumphs of my floor mates ought to be celebrated, and I do occasionally occupy this level."

"Don't be haughty," Patty said. "Admit it, you just see us all as one pathetic shit show, don't you?"

"Come now," Digy answered, "how could I possibly admit that without being haughty…but there's no reason to take that tone. There's plenty of Digy to go around."

"I wouldn't be too sure about that," Patty said. "I think Dinky might've been a more apt nickname for you."

"Ouch, this version of Patty has teeth," Digy said with a smirk.

"Watch yourself, hon," Patty replied, addressing Digy's companion. "You might think you've landed a catch, only to find out too late that these waters are poisoned."

With that Patty stormed off, zigzagging her way through the small crowd and quitting the common area.

"She certainly makes a dramatic exit," said Digy.

"At least Patty didn't slap you," she said, "or one of your henchmen might've wrestled her to the ground."

"Where are your horsemen exactly?" asked the Psycho. "Is that guy in the corner with the mustache one of them?"

"Allow me to introduce Date House's newest resident," Digy said, indicating his companion. "She's also an accomplished member of the Marine Corps. I'm told she can break a clavicle with the heel of her foot and collapse a carotid artery with her thumb."

"Impressive," said the Psycho. "Does she also speak?"

"Only when spoken to," Digy answered for her, "if only you shared that same attribute."

"Don't talk down to me from your ivory tower," barked the Psycho.

"We live in the same tower numb nuts," Digy replied equably.

"You're the second person that's called me that tonight."

"I'm sure I shan't be the last."

"You're an arrogant prick that needs to be taken down a notch or two," the Psycho said, aggressively stabbing his index finger in the direction of Digy's chest. Before the offending digit made contact with its intended target, Digy's escort snatched the Psycho's wrist, adroitly twisting it behind his back with such explosive force as to cause him to bend at the waist and yelp in pain.

"It's not that you're wrong about me," Digy said softly, "it's that you're the wrong guy to do anything about it."

"Let me go," pleaded the Psycho.

"Release him," Digy ordered.

"No," said the bodyguard, pushing the Psycho's twisted wrist against his spine, preventing him from standing up straight. "My job is to protect you—not to take orders from you. I'll have my partner remove him from this floor while I remain with you."

The man with a mustache approached and grabbed the Psycho firmly by the back of his neck. Digy's escort released his wrist.

"I'll get even with you for this," the Psycho threatened. The man with the mustache applied more pressure to his neck, causing the Psycho to bend at the waist once more as he was led out.

"How precisely?" Digy taunted. "By adding my name again to your enemies list. One day you'll have to make good on your threats if you wish to be taken seriously, though I would advise against it."

"I think that's quite enough excitement for tonight," said Digy's escort. "Let's get you someplace more secure."

"Could I impose upon you to say that in a slightly sexier way?"

"Absolutely not," said the escort as she placed her hand on her charge's shoulder and guided him out of the common area.

"Just when I was starting to have fun," Digy said to his occasional floor mates as he was led away. "Maybe they'll let me out again for spring break."

She stood alone now with no one to talk to and nothing to drink. She looked around and saw several people she recognized, but she couldn't remember any of their names. She was about to leave when her roommate reappeared.

"Where have you been?" she asked. "You missed all the excitement."

"I think I caught some of it," he said. "I passed the Psycho on the stairs being manhandled by a mustachioed man."

"What were you doing on the stairs and where's my beer?"

"You're full of questions."

"Well, you missed the Prodigy."

"Too bad, but I think this evening may still have an interesting moment yet to come."

Just then the lights went out. From the hallway could be heard ceremonial trumpets. A freshman entered the common area holding up a lit lighter and carrying a boom box. Then the Schiz entered, waving to the enraptured audience, followed by another freshman also holding a lighter and tossing confetti onto the floor behind him. Then Poopy entered, adorned in a shower curtain cinched around his neck in the style of a cape, his face looking considerably less sweaty, though still bearing the slackness that is the hallmark of being hammered. Finally the procession ended with the third freshman, who entered holding a journal high above his head in one hand and a lighter in the other.

The audience feverishly applauded their Crap King and his retinue, but the Schiz held up his outstretched hands to quiet them.

"A moment such as this requires no stilted speech or formal oration, but rather demands only your solemn silence," the Schiz said aloud. "Your somber stillness, your sepulchral shut-up-ness," the Schiz said to himself. "So without further a-doo-doo...freshmen, commence with the book burning."

The seemingly well-rehearsed trio of teenagers lined up next to the pair of trashcans. The first lit a fire in the trashcan containing paper, which had been cleansed of Poopy's contribution. The second stood at the ready near the can containing water. The third, after several attempts, lit the corner of the journal and tossed it into the smoldering can. Soon the flames grew in intensity to the top of the can, and the hushed audience appeared transfixed by the glow. The pair of fire-starting freshmen flanked the burning can, flapping towels to direct the smoke toward an open window in the hallway.

Suddenly the halcyon ceremony was interrupted by someone snapping on the lights. "Where is it?" shouted the Psycho, looking disheveled and half-crazed.

"Where's what?" he asked calmly, as the Psycho marched directly toward him.

"You know what," grunted the Psycho.

"I know you shouldn't leave your door unlocked," he said, now face to face with the Psycho, "or the middle drawer of your desk."

"Give it back to me," demanded the Psycho.

"Sure," he said, pulling a journal from his pocket, "here you go."

The Psycho grabbed the journal and examined it with confusion, opening it to the first page and reading it out loud. "'Yesterday was my twelfth birthday, and this morning my poop was the color of the German chocolate cake we had at my party.'" The Psycho was nearly apoplectic with rage. "What the hell is this?"

"Sounds like a journal entry to me," he said coolly.

"But it isn't mine!"

"No, it isn't," he confirmed. "You see, I swapped your shit list with Poopy's."

Realizing what had become of his enemies list, the Psycho scrambled to the burning trashcan. He pushed the water attendant away from his receptacle and doused the flames. The fire hissed and an acrid smoke rose from the can. The Psycho reached inside the still warm container and pulled out a handful of sodden, black ashes. The Psycho looked up, his eyes now glowing the same color as the conflagration of a moment ago.

"You're now entry one in volume two of my enemies list."

"If all you want is a number two journal," he replied, "then why don't you just keep Poopy's?"

At that moment every mouth in the common area let out a loud, fulsome laugh—every mouth save one.

Chapter Twenty

"Can I sleep with you tonight?" she asked as she changed into her nightshirt and sleeping shorts.

"I've woken up with you in my bed three times this week, so I suppose we might as well skip the morning story of how you ended up here," he said as he got into his bed. "Though I feel your bedtime company is wasted on me. There are any number of boys in this building who would be glad to have you as a sleeping companion."

"Shut up and scoot over."

"Ah, there's the pillow talk that I'm so fond of."

"Do you mind putting your arm around me...just until I fall asleep?" she asked as she snuggled next to him.

"Fine, but I draw the line at whispering sweet nothings."

"I don't even know what those are," she said as she rearranged her pillow. "Were you possibly kind of rough on the Psycho tonight?"

"It was just a jape. He got his revenge by flushing Poopy's perfect ring of poo when he left."

"Maybe...maybe not. Between you and the Prodigy mocking him, I fear you might've escalated matters."

"What did the Prodigy say to the Psycho...that sounds like the setup for an unfunny joke, doesn't it?"

"Digy's a man with no subconscious," she said, ignoring his question. "He's aware of every ephemeral thought that passes through his head and expresses each with ardor. Those of us who have gotten to know him don't take the things he says seriously, but you destroying the Psycho's journal is not something our downstairs neighbor is going to take lightly."

"What makes you say that?"

"That enemies list of his was a release valve of sorts in which he could express his feelings. You've taken that away from him in a publicly humiliating way—that coupled with Digy daring him to act...I think it might only be a matter of time until he explodes."

"That's a pretty perspicacious read on the Psycho—well done."

"Thanks, but I'm not joking. You should be careful."

"He's just a little boy who wants the world to think he's a big man...believe me, I know the type."

"Speaking of—did you hear from your father? Is he still planning to come next weekend?"

"I spoke to his nurse yesterday. According to him, my father had an up-and-down week, so I'd say he's a firm maybe for next weekend's visit."

Chapter Twenty-one

"We're not in right now, so please leave a message," said her insincerely cheery voice on the answering machine.

"If this is the dentist's office calling to confirm my appointment for tomorrow, please reschedule it for the same time next Saturday," said his sincerely cranky voice on the answering machine.

"If this is my thesis advisor, then I apologize for missing our meeting again, but I have no new updates about my project, as the subject of my paper was scheduled to visit campus this weekend, though it seems now that he won't be able to come until next weekend due to health-related issues, so maybe it would be best if we meet in two weeks. I had intended to call earlier, but—" Her voice on the machine cut off abruptly, having reached the time limit for the outgoing message.

"Who do you think it is?" she asked as she got herself ready to start her day.

"My money's on someone who's irritated at having to listen to such a long recording," he answered from his bed, reading a magazine.

Beep. "This is your thesis advisor. It's noon, and you missed our meeting...again. That's strike two. Yes, let's reschedule for a fortnight from now, so you can tell me how the interview went, and we can assess your progress before spring break begins."

"Do you think he sounded a little drunk?" she asked.

"I think he sounded a lot annoyed," he answered. "Why didn't you call to cancel your meeting rather than making us rerecord the outgoing message over and over until time ran out just as you got to the part when you invent an excuse for why you didn't call him?"

"Because I didn't have anything to report other than I didn't have anything to report, but I didn't want to lie to him by making up an excuse about why I couldn't go to the meeting."

"Then you should've left a message on his machine when he wasn't in his office," he said.

"I think he's always in his office."

"Probably not after the building closes."

"It seems a little transparent to call his office so late."

"Maybe, though perhaps he wouldn't have been as annoyed," he said. "However, it's possible I could've been hearing intoxication and not annoyance…there was that whole 'fortnight' business."

"He is an English teacher."

"Sure, but he's not English."

"Though he did make a good point," she said. "What are we going to do for spring break?"

"I don't think he made any such point, but I've been thinking of that too. If my father does come next weekend, then I'd rather not go home for a visit over our break…believe me, a little bit of the little man goes a long way."

"We should go somewhere warm then."

"A road trip is feasible," he said. "My father's nurse was going to drive him down in his car. I could drive them back and then keep my father's car until after break week. It's enormous, so we could even sleep in it if we had to."

"Sounds like a good plan to me."

"Says the person who thought it a good plan to record a highly detailed message that conveniently cuts off at the part explaining why she couldn't be bothered to make a simple phone call in the first place."

Chapter Twenty-two

Returning from her Friday afternoon meeting with her counselor, she saw Poopy as she got off the elevator on their floor.

"You don't look so good," she said. "Don't tell me you're backed up again."

"Quite the contrary," Poopy replied. "It's been a week since my perfect circle, and I haven't been able to stop pooping since."

"I'm sorry for your troubles, but that's really all the detail I need."

"You don't understand…every time I feel a toot it turns into a poop."

"Well, it's cute that you rhymed your condition, but as I mentioned you can spare me the—"

"After lunch I pooped a turd so dark that I could see the end of time in it."

"You should maybe stop studying your poops for a while," she suggested.

"I skipped all my afternoon classes because I was scared. I fear my turd may portend a malevolent event."

"Why do so few things portend pleasant events?" she asked rhetorically. "Seriously, you should just flush the toilet, then stand up and walk away."

"Perhaps you're right," Poopy said as he grabbed at his gut. "I think I'll have plenty of opportunities over the next couple of days to practice your technique."

"Please don't call it my technique, but yes…you look as if it might be in your best interest to stay close to a restroom this weekend."

"You're a font of fantastic advice," Poopy said as he continued on towards the men's room.

"That was sarcasm, right?"

"Yes," Poopy answered over his shoulder. "By the way, there's someone waiting for you outside your room."

Curious, she thought. She rounded the corner to find a diminutive, well-dressed man standing at the end of the hall in front of her door. He wore a long coat and dark sunglasses that gave him a sinister aura.

"Can I help you?" she asked as she cautiously approached.

"Perhaps you can, miss," the man replied. "I'm looking for Vivian."

"Yes, I'm Vivien."

"No, I'm sorry, I'm looking for Vivian Lee."

"Yes, that's me…Vivien Leigh."

"I think there's been some sort of mistake," the man said. "I asked at the front desk what room my son, Vivian Lee, was staying in. The young man behind the counter seemed confused by my question but then gave me this room number."

"Oh, now I understand…his name is my name too, so the front desk inadvertently gave you the correct room, which was assigned to me," Vivien explained. "You're my roommate's father…I can see the resemblance. You two share the same chin."

"I didn't know my son lived with a woman."

"Well, he was assigned a different room, though I suspect the front desk hasn't updated its room listings since last semester anyway," she said as she unlocked her door, "but it worked out for both of us that he stay with me instead."

"I'm not sure I follow, but then that happens to me a lot where my son is concerned."

"Please come in, and I'll try to explain it better." She entered the dorm room and pulled out her roommate's desk chair for him to have a seat. She then went around the room picking up dirty socks and other dorm room debris. "See my mother married a 'Leigh,' and one of her favorite movies is *A Streetcar Named Desire*, so she thought it would be fun to name me after the actress who played Blanche DuBois."

She paused in the middle of the room, holding her unwashed undergarments and empty food wrappers. "I probably don't need to go back quite that far."

"That's fine miss…take your time," said the father, folding his coat and laying it over the back of the chair. "I myself was named after an English explorer."

"Isn't that interesting?" she asked as she studied her roommate's father. "You know, you look younger than I imagined."

"Thanks, my outsides are healthier than my insides. Please forgive the sunglasses; my eyes have developed a sensitivity to light, so if I don't wear them I get headaches."

"I have fabric sensitivity. My closet is full of clothes that I never wear…I usually just dress in the same three outfits over and over."

"So how did you and my son meet?"

"At the start of the spring semester student mixer," she answered. "We hit it off right away and having the same name—though spelled differently—made our meeting seem like serendipity."

"So you two aren't together then?"

"No dad," said said Vivian Jr. from the doorway of the dorm room, "your son's still gay."

"Let's not start this," said Vivian Sr. as he stood. "I was only asking a question."

The two approached one another, shaking hands in the center of the room.

"When I spoke to your nurse yesterday, he told me you hadn't been feeling well and that you probably weren't going to make it for your visit this weekend."

"How many times do I have to remind you, Robert's not my nurse…he's an old boxing buddy, who also happens to be a healthcare provider, and he checks on me a couple of times a week."

"Fine," said Vivian Jr. as he gave his roommate a knowing look.

"I woke up this morning feeling better than I had in a long while, and then Robert had a family emergency come up, so we decided that he would drop me off here, and he'd take my car downstate to visit his family."

"But I wanted the car for spring break."

"He'll be back on Sunday to pick me up. You can drive us home and keep my car for the next couple of weeks."

"I'm so pleased everything will work out for Robert."

"Why are you upset?" asked Vivian Sr. "He called early this afternoon and left a message that we were coming."

"I've been on campus all afternoon and haven't had a chance to check the machine."

"Will my visit disrupt plans you've made since you last spoke to Robert?"

"I have a dentist appointment tomorrow…though I suppose I can reschedule it."

"Good then," said Vivian the Elder, putting on his coat again. "I'm staying at the hotel on campus. Do you mind walking me back there? I had thought I might take a stroll around my old stomping grounds, but suddenly I'm feeling rather tired."

"Sure dad, I'll walk you."

"Let me rest for an hour or so and then perhaps we can all have dinner tonight. Will your enchanting roommate be able to join us?"

"She will," Vivien answered. "In fact, if you don't mind, I'd like to ask you some questions about your time here as a student athlete."

"I'd be delighted to answer any question from someone as captivating as you."

"Your father is quite the charmer."

"All right you two," said Vivian the Younger as he escorted his father from the room, "let's save some of the pleasantries for dinner."

Chapter Twenty-three

Vivien had done so many things since her roommate and his father left, and yet it seemed as if she had accomplished almost nothing. She had cleaned the room, which mostly consisted of picking up her discarded items that should have been thrown out ages ago, but the room still looked shabby. She had tried on the four dresses from the back of her closet, but none of them fit quite right, each of them either being too snug in one place or too loose in another, and all of them had seams that irritated her skin, so she was still wearing the same jeans and sweatshirt from before.

She'd also thought of questions she might ask Vivian Sr. over dinner, even writing a few of them down, but they all seemed so banal. He had been such an amiable gentleman, not at all like the homophobic ogre she had envisioned from her roommate's description, that she didn't want to ask any incendiary questions, such as whether he felt the university—an institution putatively committed to developing minds—should be held accountable for facilitating the long-term destruction of his.

The room had grown dark, so she turned on the overhead light, which always felt too bright to her. Looking up at it, she noticed several dead flies in the light fixture. She moved her chair to the middle of the room, stood on it, and reached up toward the fixture. Her fingertips could only extend up to the edges of the diffuser, but after straining several times she was able to lift the plastic piece enough to remove it from its metal mount.

She stepped down to the floor and looked inside the semitransparent, rectangle-shaped diffuser—five dead flies, all with their little legs in the air. She wondered why they turned over that way. Was their final instinct to lay on their backs and wait for death, or did they die upright and then tip over from top-heaviness due to their wings after their feet lost stickiness? She thought that to someone else the dead bugs might've seemed a lugubrious tableau, but to her thinking they had probably achieved their life's ambition to find the source of light in their universe and so had likely died with a sense of satisfaction at having completed their quest, if flies were in fact capable of such thoughts, which she figured likely.

She took the diffuser to the wastebasket near her desk, tilted it in at an angle, and used one of Vivian's magazines to scrape the fly carcasses into the trash. She wiped the edge of the magazine with yet another of her dirty socks that she found behind the wastebasket and then tossed the magazine back onto her roommate's bed—an efficient if not ceremonial sendoff.

The phone rang. She considered letting the machine answer it, but then she didn't want to wait through the interminable outgoing message to find out who was calling, so she picked up.

"Hello."

"Vivien?" a whispering voice asked.

"Yes, who is this?"

"It's me, Vivian…your roommate."

"Oh sorry," she said. "I didn't recognize your voice. I don't think we've ever actually spoken over the phone before, and for some reason it sounds strange to hear you say my name."

"Listen, I apologize, but I don't think it's a good idea if we have dinner tonight."

"Is everything okay?" she asked. "Was your dad able to take a nap?"

"When we got back to his hotel room he had that far-off look in his eyes that he gets just before he has an episode. Ever since then he's been all rage and vitriol. I think he overdid it today."

"I'm sorry to hear that. Is there anything I can do?"

"No…thanks," he whispered. "I finally got him calmed down. I think I'll wait here until he falls asleep. Once he tires himself out, he usually sleeps like the dead and then wakes up feeling better in the morning. I'll probably be back later. I just didn't want you to worry."

"I'm glad you called."

"Sure…maybe we can try again for dinner tomorrow."

"I'd like that."

Chapter Twenty-four

Vivien only ever remembered her dreams when they were interrupted. It was pitch black. She heard the jangling of far off wind chimes. Otherwise, all was silent. She could sense someone moving nearby...above her maybe. She strained to listen and to see, but there was only the sound of quietly clinking metal and darkness. She thought maybe her eyes no longer worked. She shouted at the person hovering close by and discovered that her voice no longer worked either. She felt a hand on the back of neck...and then another over her mouth. She should've been terrified but found it funny that her assailant was trying to keep a mute person from screaming. As she reached up to grab the hands, two more stopped her, seizing her wrists. Okay, this is weird.

"What's weird?" Vivian asked as he opened the door. The light from the hallway backlit him so that she could only see his silhouette in the dimness of their dorm room.

"I was having a dream."

"Anything saucy?" he asked.

"No, it was stupid...probably just a reaction to hearing your key in the door," she said, sitting up in her bed.

He closed their door and walked between the two beds, bumping into the desk chair in the center of the dark room.

"What is this doing here?"

"The chair? I don't know...sitting, or standing, or laying perhaps. What do chairs do? It sounds peculiar to say resting, though I suppose they perform their primary function in a resting state."

"Why is it in the middle of the floor?" he clarified.

"It assisted me earlier with an insect memorial service. How's your father?"

"He's asleep. He took some medicine, so he'll sleep until midmorning at least."

"What time is it now?"

"Early morning. Do you mind if I sleep with you?" he asked as he took off his jacket.

"In my bed? That's quite a change. I should warn you that I haven't washed these sheets in a while."

"I could fall asleep on sandpaper right now," he said as he got into bed with her. "Can I hold you?"

"Sure, you know I like that."

She could feel his hands exploring her backside. They moved with uncertainty, as if probing for some new place to be.

"That's more groping than holding," she said.

"Does it bother you?"

"I don't do that...we don't do that together—that's not who we are."

"You're right...this was wrong of me," he said, rising from her bed and getting into his own.

"You don't have to leave...just cut it out with the roamin' hands and rushin' fingers."

"No, I should sleep alone tonight," he said. "I'm just in a strange place right now with my father."

"Attempting to be the man he wants you to be?" she asked.

"Yes...that's quite insightful by the way."

"Thanks, I have a good tutor, but I still don't understand why you'd try to be like someone who you have so much contempt for?"

"If you can answer that for me then I'll make you my tutor."

Chapter Twenty-five

When she woke up he was gone. *He must've only slept for a few hours before he left again*, she thought. "But didn't he say that his father would likely sleep until at least midmorning?" she asked herself aloud. She felt conflicting impulses to leave the room and to stay put. Lately her dorm room felt smaller the longer she inhabited it, but somehow she also felt more connected to her roommate when she occupied the space they shared, even if he wasn't there. She decided to go to the restroom to brush her teeth.

In the hallway, she saw one of the horsemen standing outside the men's room. *Digy must be staying on the floor*, she figured. She wondered if it would make her happier or sadder to be so important that bodyguards were employed to protect her, but then she couldn't decide if she was happy or sad at that very moment, so the issue seemed moot. All she knew for sure was that when she ran her tongue across the front of her teeth they felt like they were growing moss.

When she returned to her dorm room she saw the blinking light of the answering machine indicating a new message. "I was out of the room for like two minutes," she said to herself as she pressed the button to listen to the message.

"Hey, it's me. I wanted to get over to the hotel before my father woke up, but he's still asleep, so I've just been hanging around here. We're going to tour a bit of the campus later... check out his old boxing gym, which I think is now a yoga studio—so that should be a quite surprise for the old man. We'll stop by the dorm afterwards, but don't feel like you have to wait around. Uh...sorry again for any confusion I may have caused last night."

She resisted the urge to replay the message and parse every possible meaning of each of his statements—not because she felt giving quarter to the neurotic impulse was futile and counterproductive, but rather because she still didn't trust her ability to infer subtext and allusion.

She wished that she was tired so she'd have a reason to go back to bed. Then she wished that she was hungry so she'd have a reason to go downstairs to the cafeteria. But she was neither, so she decided to sit quietly at her desk and listen for wind chimes. Instead she heard the humming of the ceiling light. The hum was hardly noticeable at first, but as she focused on the noise it grew louder until it became a strident buzzing that was impossible to ignore. She reasoned that she hadn't reaffixed the diffuser properly in its metal mount the night before. Then, without warning, she was assaulted by a sound so stentorian that she leapt out her chair.

The downstairs neighbor was playing his hate rock at full volume. "Why is such an earsplitting stereo even allowed in the dorms?" she asked herself. She stomped on the floor with all the force her flip-flopped feet could produce. The sound from below instantly ceased. All was quiet, but it took a few moments for her to hear the humming of the overhead light again.

Then she heard another, softer sound coming from below...a faint tapping. She got down on her hands and knees to listen, but she didn't hear it anymore. She put her ear to the floor and after several seconds she heard it again: tap, tap, tap. Was the Psycho sending her a message in Morse code? She knocked on the floor three times with her knuckles. Another tap, tap, tap was the response.

She didn't know whether the Psycho was trying to say, "I love you" or "go to hell"…maybe he was simply telling her "I am here." She turned over onto her back, looking up at the ceiling light. She wondered what her downstairs neighbor was thinking and then what her roommate was thinking. Her thoughts about the two of them blurred until their motives intersected.

Chapter Twenty-six

"Did you fall out of bed?" asked Vivian as he stood in the doorway looking down at her.

"That's a silly question," Vivien said as she drowsily opened her eyes.

"Given the situation, I don't think it is," he said as he slowly opened the door all the way, making sure it wouldn't hit the top of her head.

"There's no situation here," she said defensively. "I simply happened to be thinking weighty thoughts of such immense gravity that it seemed safest to do so from the lowest point in the room."

"Weighty thoughts that caused you to fall sleep."

"Well I'm awake now, so help me up," she demanded as she held up a hand for assistance.

He grasped her hand and helped her to her feet. She brushed herself off and fussed with her hair.

"Where's your dad?"

"He's in the restroom," he answered. "We're going to have dinner soon. You still want to come?"

"Sure, what time is it?"

"It's only 4:30, but you know old people...they like to eat early."

"Your dad's not that old. How was the campus tour?"

"Terrible…he complained about everything—mostly me. The worst part about his forgetfulness is that he repeats the same criticisms over and over. I miss the days when his disparaging remarks had a bit of originality."

"I'm sorry you didn't have a better time. I'd hoped you two would find some common ground on campus."

"The only thing we have in common is that neither of us can stand the other."

"That's surprising."

"How so?" he asked.

"I only spoke to him for a few minutes yesterday, but he seemed to have a real warmth about him."

"Don't let him fool you—it's his anger that keeps him warm."

"Maybe I misread him then," she said. "Perhaps I'm not making as much progress as I thought."

"Don't be too hard on yourself. He can be tricky to read. He's like an old blues song: what he isn't saying is more important than what he is. He excels at expressing disapproval through silence."

"Is it possible that he isn't expressing disapproval at all then?"

"Shh," Vivian whispered as he furtively looked out into the hallway. "He's coming."

"Then you should probably stop whispering and just talk about something else."

"What should we talk about?" he asked.

"Anything you want."

"But like what though?"

"What are you two talking about?" asked Vivian Sr. as he stood in the doorway.

The roommates looked at each other as if to telepathically choose a suitable topic of conversation since they had been unable to pick one out loud. Finally Vivien blurted out, "weather."

"Yes," Vivian Jr. confirmed, "Vivien was trying to decide whether or not she would come with us to dinner."

"I do hope you'll join us. Since my wife passed, I so rarely have an opportunity to spend time in the company of a beguiling woman."

"Okay," said Vivian Jr., "while you two figure out where we're going to have our early-bird dinner, I'll visit the facilities."

The father moved into the dorm room to give his son a wide berth through the doorway. The son stepped into the hallway and vanished from view.

"He's never mentioned his mom," said Vivien. "Were they close?"

"As close as any mother and child can be," replied Vivian, "but she died when he was very young, so I don't think he remembers much about her...only that there was once someone who loved him the way only a mother could and then there wasn't. I wonder sometimes how he would be different today if she was still alive and it had been me who'd taken ill with cancer."

"You mean you wonder if your son would still be gay?" The question had formed and been uttered before she had a chance to filter it. It hung in the air between them, making the tiny room feel all the tinier. She wanted to take the question back almost as much as she wanted an answer.

"I can see why my son likes you so much." Vivian's mouth curled into a smile.

"We're not romantic," she said. "You do know that your son is a homosexual, don't you?"

"Of course I know. I've known since he was in junior high. I admit that I didn't handle it well at first, but only because I didn't want his life to be any harder than it had to be."

Vivian entered the men's restroom, turned the hot water handle of the closest sink, and looked at himself in the long mirror. No other sink was in use, either in his row of four or the row on the wall behind him. In his periphery he saw the reflection of the back of his head in the mirror opposite of his that spanned the other four sinks. He turned his head left and then right to see his chin and the tip of his nose. From this perspective, he looked like a stranger to himself. The parallel mirrors created an infinity effect, an endless tunnel of his repeated self with his back turned.

He was startled from his reverie by the flushing of a toilet. He had thought he was alone in the restroom. Suddenly a large man in a boxy suit came from around the corner. The man appeared too quickly to have pulled up his pants or buckled his belt after using the toilet. Vivian wondered if the man was simply announcing his presence with the flush. He didn't seem to be in a hurry to wash his hands. Rather he stood statue still just beyond the bank of sinks, staring at nothing while at the same time watching Vivian. The longer the man stood there, the more Vivian's anxiety grew. Vivian splashed his face with water that was now too hot. He turned off the water and was about to make a hasty exit with a wet, warm face when he heard a stall door close. An ectomorphic, pimply-faced teenager rounded the corner, walking with the confidence of an emperor. Now Vivian understood.

"I love my son very much," Vivian Sr. said as if confessing to his son's roommate, "and I tell him so as often as I can, but he just doesn't hear me."

"Maybe it's drowned out by your belittling comments," she replied. "Or maybe because of those comments he's learned to take everything you say with a grain of sand."

"I think you mean grain of salt, and I don't belittle my son. I've made a few remarks over the years about some of his past boyfriends, but only because I didn't think they were good enough for him. As a cop you develop a sense for who can and can't be trusted…it isn't always correct, but it usually is."

"Is it possible that you say the hurtful things your son has mentioned when you're not lucid?"

"Lucid?" Vivian Sr. asked with surprise. "What has my son told you about my condition?"

"That you have a form of dementia which resulted from boxing."

"I took some pretty good lumps when I boxed that may have slowed me down some, but I don't have dementia."

"Vivian told me you had to retire from the police force."

"That's true, but not because of dementia. Doctors call what I have chronic fatigue syndrome. I do have occasional lapses of memory and sometimes find it hard to concentrate, which is why I can't drive anymore."

"That's it?"

"Don't sound so disappointed. I also have persistent joint and muscle pain, and sometimes for no reason at all I get so exhausted that I can't get out of bed…but I haven't lost my mind."

"Wouldn't someone who's lost his mind think that?" Vivien asked.

"Exactly, which is how I know I haven't lost my mind, because I realize that I'm losing my mind…slowly. I'm friends with enough old boxers to understand the thing about having lost your mind is that you're the only one who doesn't realize it's gone. That's not me. I misplace my house key more often

125

than I care to admit, but I haven't forgotten where I live…at least not yet."

Vivien thought through the tortuous but flawless logic and agreed that it made sense, but then she found herself even more confused.

"It seems my son wasn't completely truthful about my condition," said Vivian Sr. "So what did he tell you about his?"

"You're the one they call the Prodigy, right?" asked Vivian. "I'm a big fan…well, not so much a fan, but I've heard of you."

Digy smirked without looking up from the sink as he washed his hands with the fastidiousness of a surgeon.

"What is it that you do again…spend all day reading the dictionary? Seems like a colossal waste of time."

Digy continued to wash his hands in silence.

"Are you just trying to learn new words to make yourself sound smarter? What version of the dictionary do you use anyway…Webster's?"

Digy turned off the faucet and flicked the water dripping from his hands into the sink's bowl. His bodyguard handed him a paper towel from the dispenser on the wall.

"That's a neat trick," Vivian said. "Will he fetch your slippers too? Nothing to say, huh? What are you, like one of those towering figures who doesn't speak…you know, the inflatable characters who twist in the wind, advertising for used-car lots while blighting urban roadways."

Digy dried his hands and said to his bodyguard, "This is precisely the type of invidious outcome I predicted when the residence hall director countermanded my privacy in the restroom policy after that Psycho fellow filed a formal complaint."

"Would you like me to get rid of him?" asked the body-guard.

"No, much to my dismay, it's a free country in which anyone has the right to speak his mind, or at least what passes for one."

"So you can talk," said Vivian, turning to face Digy who now stood in the center of the room. "By the way, I thought you usually had a pair of henchmen hovering around you. Where's the Tweedle Dee that goes with this Tweedle Dum?"

"In answer to your last question, Ms. Dee is seeing to the transportation arrangements for my dinner engagement this evening."

"Are you going out to eat too? Maybe we could join you."

"Not unless you're on the guest list, which you aren't. You see, it's a plenary event...I'm sure you understand. In answer to your first question: yes, when some speak of me they use the sobriquet "the Prodigy," though I abhor it. In answer to your second question, I study the dictionary...I don't merely read it as one might read a magazine. I assume your third question was rhetorical. The answer to your fourth question, the one about what dictionary I use, in case you've lost track, is the OED; I am privy to a prototype, Internet edition currently under development that is scheduled for release next year. Your remaining questions were simply meant to derogate, so I won't bother answering them."

"You're like the guy who says without 'further ado,' and then proceeds to talk for a half-hour, aren't you?"

"As I told you: your questions aren't worth the bother. Now if you'll excuse me, I do have that engagement."

"Wait, hang on...you mentioned the Oxford English Dictionary. I didn't realize it was going online, but then I guess soon everything will be."

"Are you sure that's his diagnosis?" Vivien asked skeptically.

"I'm afraid so. The doctors think it has to do with losing his mother when he did. They say if he'd lost her earlier, he wouldn't remember her at all, and if he'd lost her later, then he would've been better able to cope. But, I can't help thinking that it was somehow my fault. I did the best I could with him, but I lost my mother when I wasn't much older than him, so I know how that hurt can affect you."

"Then you were brought up by your father too?"

"I'm not sure I'd say he brought me up. He was a rotten man—sometimes he wouldn't even feed me—but he's the reason I was such a good fighter."

"He taught you how to box?" she asked.

"He taught me how to take a punch. I was the rare boxer who could compete without being angry that my opponent was trying to hurt me or afraid that he would succeed. No one I faced was ever as mean as my father when he was drunk and wanted to go a few rounds. That gave me an advantage in the ring, because until then I'd never gotten a fair fight in which I could hit back."

"That sounds like an awful way to grow up."

"I promised myself no matter how difficult being a single father was that I would never lay a hand on my son to hurt him. I kept that promise, but even so Vivian grew up to resent me the same way I resented my father."

"It doesn't sound like that has anything to do with how you raised him," she said.

"I never hit him, but…I don't know, I'm sure there were things that I could've done differently…done better."

"I imagine every parent feels that way."

"Maybe…but my son has had a harder life than most people his age. Being on campus again, I can't help but think how it was for me back then. When I left for college, I finally got away from my father's abuse, but I never really stopped being afraid of him until he died my senior year. It wasn't until then that I felt like a man rather than a boy living in his shadow. I think the same thing about Vivian now...like he can't be the man he was meant to be until I'm gone."

"I wish you knew how much he looks up to you."

"I do know," Vivian Sr. said, "but from that perspective all he sees is me looking down at him...no matter how many times I tell him that I put him above everything else. He's a lot like me, you know...a brawler, but he doesn't fight with his fists—instead he uses his wits, which makes me proud."

"I had imagined you flipping through the dictionary and crossing out words you didn't like with a crayon," Vivian Jr. said, "but you're using computers...that sounds way more official than I gave you credit for."

"I see, of course, that you're mocking my work, but I can also see that you're curious about it. My process is to write notes for edits that I believe would make our language more concise and comprehensible, increasing its appeal as a candidate for a common, global language. I mean really, how can the world's populations be expected to evolve together if we can't even talk to one another without the intrusion of a translator?"

"And your efforts to make English the front runner for a universal language would give native speakers the upper hand in global affairs, which is why you get funding for your little project and your own private goon squad."

"Everyone would benefit from a single, simpler language...but indeed some would benefit more."

"So give me an example of what you do," Vivian said.

"I'm in the P's right now, or more specifically the Pu's. Today I wrote a lengthy recommendation, supported by research and cross-referenced with contemporary usage indices, to expunge the words 'Puissant' and 'Pusillanimous.' Do you know what either of those mean?"

"Sure, one is an adjective describing you—pusillanimous means fainthearted—and the other is an adjective describing me—puissant means mighty."

"Very good," Digy said. "I disagree with your assessments of course, but I'm impressed by your familiarity with unfamiliar words. I've found those two words have a usage far below the benchmark that I contend should be the standard for a new, more efficient English. Each can easily be substituted with synonyms that are more commonly understood, such as timid and powerful."

"So you want to discard them simply because they're underused? P.U. is right. What about the richness that comes from variety…not just from English but of having many different languages to express our ideas? Who gave you the authority to make those decisions?"

"The federal government," Digy answered. "My work is important for our country. You know, you sound to me like a poet; a truly pointless discipline that would suit someone like you."

"What makes your thoughts more important than mine? After all, we attend the same university, and there are more elite schools than ours. Maybe at one of those better colleges there's some jackass like you working on the same project, but he has all the advantages of doing so at a more prestigious institution."

"I would know if that were the case," Digy said.

"Would you, or would the government put you on display, showing off how smart you are while they hedged their bets with someone even smarter working in secret? If your project is so important, then maybe it's too important for them to put all their egos in one basket."

"You see," Vivian Sr. said on the verge of tears, "my father killed himself."

"I'm sorry," Vivien replied.

"Don't be, it was the best thing he ever did for me. There weren't many people at the funeral, and the family that did come didn't seem particularly upset. An aunt told me my father committed suicide because he was lonely...first he'd become estranged from his family, then he'd lost his wife, and then I went away to college. I never thought I meant anything to him—he sure didn't show it—but I couldn't help but be pleased by the possibility that I was partially responsible for him taking his life...I've never told anyone that before."

"I'm easy to talk to that way. I don't exhibit the same emotions as most people—or even have the same emotions, as far as I know—so I don't give off the sense that I'm judging what I'm being told, but you still get the relief of unburdening... sort of like confessing to a priest who doesn't understand your language."

"I think you have a gift for connecting with people... maybe because you're a naturally open person, unlike the rest of us who have to work so hard at it...or maybe it's just because all my friends are old cops and old boxers who ain't so good at talking about what they're thinking. Either way, thanks for listening."

"You're welcome. Vivian would be pleased by your compliment about my openness, even if I don't quite know what you mean. If you don't my saying, I've never understood the stigma associated with suicide…after all, there's no shame in walking out of a bad movie or folding a losing hand in poker…and don't they throw in the towel when a boxing match isn't going well?"

"I never did, even when I probably should have, but I see your point. I boxed to prove that I could live life on my own terms…now that's been taken from me, so a quick exit would make more sense than a long one, but I never wanted to be anything except the exact opposite of my father, so the thought of killing myself the way he did is out of the question, even though it would be easier on me and better for my son. It makes me sick to think that my stubbornness is hurting him."

"I must say that I've enjoyed our tetchy little tête-à-tête," Digy said as he adjusted his collar in the mirror, "but I am running late, so I must bid you adieu."

"I find it ironic that you think English has too many words and yet you borrow from the French to say goodbye. Speaking of French, do me a favor…since you're in the P's, don't delete my favorite word."

"Which is?"

"Portmanteau," Vivian answered.

"Ah, portmanteau…a blending of words to create a new word, like smoke and fog to create smog. Its very definition is antipodal to my efforts to attenuate our lexicon, but as it happens it's one of my favorite words too, and since it has no direct synonyms, you may consider it safe." Digy turned his back to Vivian and walked toward the exit with his bodyguard following closely behind.

"That's a relief," said Vivian, looking at himself in the mirror. "I first fell in love with the word when I learned that it's a portmanteau itself."

Digy froze in the doorway, his bodyguard nearly bumping into him. He turned back toward Vivian, motioning for his bodyguard to move out of his way. "As you alluded, the word 'portmanteau' is French in origin. It's comprised of the words porter, which translates as to carry, and manteau, which translates as cloak. Today it means a coat rack of sorts, but in 1871, the year Lewis Carroll's *Through the Looking-Glass* was first published, in which Humpty Dumpty explains to Alice how words can be combined to form new words known as portmanteaus, such as miserable and flimsy to make mimsy, a portmanteau meant a suitcase with two sides."

"That's fascinating," said Vivian, not turning away from his reflection in the mirror, "but I was referring to the independent, American origin of portmanteau."

For perhaps the first time in his young life, Digy felt flummoxed. "You must be mistaken."

"No, I'm quite certain I'm correct," Vivian said with equanimity. "I'm aware of the origin you just described, and you summarized it very succinctly, so top marks for that, but the word 'portmanteau' was also created here in the states, some years before Carroll ever recounted the Jabberwock's death, and thus quite separately. It comes from an early American drinking song, in which a young man filled with wanderlust wrestles with whether he wants to become a surveyor and explore the unmapped lands of the new country or a roustabout in hopes of getting work on a ship that explores her uncharted waterways. Ultimately he decides to become both a plateau man and a port man, as the two occupations are referred to in later verses for rhyming purposes...and so the word portmanteau was born by merging those two professions, both as a way to encapsulate the once popular song's dilemma and also to sum up its solution."

"That's...I've not heard that before."

"The song?" asked Vivian as he walked past Digy toward the door. "Nor have I or anyone else living. An old classics professor of mine told me about it. He'd come across oral accounts of the American portmanteau when he wrote his dissertation way back when. He died last year. Don't you find it poignant how seemingly trivial pieces of our language can be lost to history because they weren't valued in their time, only to have them later become imbued with significance by virtue of their absence? Anyway, I'm sure you can find an account of the portmanteau song somewhere, if you look hard enough... after all, how many early American drinking songs could there have been?"

"But why is there no account of what you've told me in the OED?" Digy meekly asked.

Vivian stood in the doorway and thought for a moment. "Who knows? Maybe the Brits are still pissed that so much of their precious dictionary was first written by a deranged American and they wanted to keep the provenance of portmanteau for themselves...well, adios."

Chapter Twenty-seven

Vivian returned to the dorm room, pleased with himself and looking forward to dinner. He opened the door to find his roommate, as he had many times before, alone and staring out the window.

"Where has my dad gotten off to now?"

"He's in the stairwell on the landing between our floor and the one below us."

"What's he doing down there?" he asked as he flopped onto his bed.

"It's where he died."

"That's a shame...did you two decide where we're going to eat?"

"No, we didn't talk about that," she answered.

"I just met the so-called Prodigy in the bathroom...what a fool. I told him a fictive story that'll send him off researching on a wild goose chase. How can we live in a world where a clown like that is regarded as exceptional and something as exquisite as key lime pie is considered commonplace? Speaking of which, we should go someplace that has really good desserts. Maybe that's all I'll order for dinner...just different slices of pie. I'm starving...did my dad say if he'd be back soon?"

"He's not coming back," she said. "He's dead."

"I think we need to spend some more time working on your sense of humor...you've told me twice now that my father's dead, and I still don't get the joke."

"It was important to him that you know he didn't kill himself."

Vivian realized that his roommate hadn't looked at him when he entered their room or at any point since then, which was both out of character and a sign that she knew it could only be him and not his father who had come through the door a moment ago. He sat up on his bed and looked at her more closely. Nothing was amiss; her clothes and hair looked the same—everything about her was as it had been before he left for the restroom, but he sensed something had changed...and yet he didn't notice anything different about her other than she wasn't making eye contact.

Vivian stood and slowly approached his roommate with a cautiousness that he neither understood nor was he fully conscious of. As he drew closer, he could see from the hairs that raised on the back of her neck that she was aware of his proximity, but still she didn't turn away from the window.

He reached out for her, putting his arms around her as he sometimes did when they slept together. She did not attempt to evade his embrace, though she didn't turn to face him either. He moved her body away from the window towards him and looked into her eyes. She met his gaze. Her eyes showed sorrow but no tears, as if she had recently become aware of a calamity that occurred in a faraway country in which she knew no one personally.

Vivian left their room and walked briskly down the hall to the stairwell door. He pushed through the door and quickly descended the stairs to the intermediate landing below. His father lay dead there just as his roommate had told him. Vivian Sr. looked broken but peaceful, as if he'd lost a big fight but was glad to have fought it. Unsure of what to do in that moment or any moment after, Vivian did what many do when suddenly faced with unexpected and upsetting circumstances…he recalled a catalog of similar scenes from movies he'd seen. He thought he should close his father's eyelids as he'd seen soldiers do in war films when a comrade was killed, but his eyes were already shut. He thought of covering his father's body like he'd seen in Westerns when an innocent man was murdered, but he decided not to retrieve a blanket from his room as being spotted with it in the hallway would be incriminating. Then he thought of the countless crime dramas he had seen and concluded that it was better not to touch the body at all.

Vivian labored to ascend the steps back to his floor, weighted as he was with the burden of what would come next. He considered many things as he returned to the dorm room, but foremost in his mind was Vivien.

He entered their room to find her laying on his bed with her face against the wall. He laid down next to her and wrapped his arms around her waist. The muscles in her back felt tense, and he couldn't help but imagine that he was holding a large, puissant python that might decide at any moment to wrap itself around him instead, but rather than slithering around to face him, she simply asked, "Did you see him?"

He thought he heard the question echo back and forth between the institutional beige walls of their room, but then it seemed more likely to him that the reverberation of the words was only in his mind. "I did…why did you…?"

"Because he wished it," she answered, "and because you wanted it."

"My father didn't have a death wish, and I certainly didn't want him dead." He heard himself pronounce the word certainly with the sibilant hiss of a snake, and he wondered now which of them was the serpent.

"My father has dementia," he said. "He doesn't know what he's saying most of the time."

"Your father doesn't have dementia."

"Really, so my father asking you to push him down the stairs was the request of a person in his right mind?"

"He didn't ask me to do it...at least, not in so many words."

"So you—who can't even identify sarcasm half the time—discerned that he wanted you to push him down those stairs to his death."

"It was a read that only someone like me could make."

"And an action only someone like you could execute?"

She twisted her body around so that she was facing him, almost touching his nose with hers. "Yes, I intuited your father's wish by listening to what he wasn't saying, as you instructed. Then I took your advice and let the problem become the solution. We walked hand in hand to the stairwell. Now your father is at peace, and you can live your life out from under his shadow the way he wanted."

"And what about you?" he asked.

"I understand that my actions have consequences," she answered. "Prison is fine for me...it won't be so very different from college. Remember, I'm the girl who likes to spend her vacations locked up by herself. Maybe they'll let me serve my sentence in solitary confinement. Besides, I don't have plans after graduation anyway."

"Don't try to be cute...this is not okay with me."

"It doesn't have to be," she consoled, "at least not right now, but someday it will be for you, and then I'll spend the rest of my life knowing I helped the only person I ever really cared about."

He grabbed her arms and pinned her underneath him. "Stop talking like this. What you did was...why are you being so damn calm? You're as crazy as my father."

"None of us are crazy…we just have different perspectives," she said. "By the way, you're hurting me."

He let go and laid back down beside her on the bed, looking up at the ceiling. "I don't know…maybe what you're saying and even what you did make some sort of sense, but the part you haven't considered is that it'll be impossible for me to live my life knowing that you're locked up for trying to help me—even if it doesn't bother you. I'm going to tell the police I killed him."

"No, you'll ruin everything," she protested. "I won't let you."

"There's nothing you can do to stop me," he said. "Unlike you, I actually have a motive for killing my father. I lied to you about my condition…it's not an excess of empathy—I think you have more of that than anyone I've ever met, at least of a certain kind. As for me, I suffer from emotional hypersensitivity of sorts. I only ever hear my father saying terrible things about me, even though everyone, including my doctors, has told me that the awful things I remember him saying aren't real. It won't take much to convince anyone who reads my file that my condition finally caused me to snap. If you try to tell the police differently, they'll pull your file and find who knows what. I'll fill in the blanks and explain that you fell in love with me and are just trying to protect me by confessing, which is more or less the truth…at least in an astigmatic way."

They held each other once more, both thinking they might never be able to do so again. She stared at him, and he continued to stare upwards. The phone rang. He got up to answer it, wanting to face the inevitable on his own terms.

"Hello."

She heard an angry, authoritative voice coming through the receiver, but she couldn't make out any of the words. Finally the voice went silent, as if it were waiting for Vivian to answer. "Yes, I'll see you then."

He hung up the phone and returned to bed.

"Was it the police?"

"No, it was my dentist," he answered. "I promised him I would be at my next appointment."

"Then maybe we still have some time."

"For what?" he asked.

"To let our problem become the solution," she answered.

"You know that has yet to actually work for either of us."

Chapter Twenty-eight

Vivien knocked on the Psycho's door. "Who the hell is it?" he demanded over his grunting music.

"It's me," she answered without raising her voice. Quickly the noise stopped and was replaced by the click of his door being unlocked.

"Hello," he said as he opened the door. "Was my music too loud again?"

"Yes, but I'm not here because of that."

"Do you want to—"

"Listen, you know I'm weird, right?" she asked.

"That's the reason I like you so much," he said as he stared at his crummy sneakers. "You're different from the other girls."

"In that case I have an offer for you, but let me warn you that you should probably say no."

"I'd never say no to you."

"Then meet me where we kissed last time…in like two minutes. I want to pick up where we left off."

"I'll be there."

"And wear a tie," she said as she turned to leave. "I want you looking your best since I'll be able to see you this time."

They Psycho watched intently as she walked down the hallway, shooting him a come-hither look over her shoulder as she entered the stairwell. Then he set to hurriedly searching for a tie. He rapidly unpacked half of his tiny closet, throwing garments into the air like rice at a wedding, but he could not locate a tie. He pulled out his suitcase from under his bed, and though packed with the clothes he almost never wore, he could not find a tie there either.

He put on a collared shirt and a pair of nicer shoes and left his room without delay. He knocked on his neighbor's door as he tucked in his shirt. "What in the world do you want?" asked his neighbor, a towering baritone from the Glee Club who learned to sing in his church choir on the Southside of Chicago at his doctor's suggestion in hopes of mitigating his violent outbursts.

"I need to borrow a tie."

"Why, you got a KKK cotillion to go to?"

"I'm not a racist," the Psycho answered. "I hate all people equally."

"Then maybe a neo-Nazi formal?"

"I'm not a Nazi either...I despise Nazis as much as everyone else. I see you wearing ties all the time when you go to your performances. Can I please borrow one?"

"You know I can't stand your music, right?"

"I feel the same way about your music," the Psycho said.

"That makes my proposal all the better. I can see you're desperate for a tie—which I find hilarious, since you usually wear ratty T-shirts and raggedy sweatpants—so I'm going to lend you a tie on the condition that you don't play your horrible music for a week and that you come to the Glee Club's Spring-tacular concert on Tuesday."

"That sounds awful, but it's a deal. Can I have the tie now?"

"Here you go," he said, handing over his least favorite tie from the rack hanging on the back of his door. "You need help tying that…it's a different kind of knot from the nooses that you're probably used to."

"No, it's fine," said the Psycho, snatching the tie as he scampered down the hall. "And I'm not a Klan member."

The Psycho reached the stairwell door, flipped up his collar, placing the middle of the tie on the back of his neck. He folded the collar down again but then realized he was breathing too heavily to button the top button of his shirt, so he let the two ends of the tie hang down his shirtfront, thinking that Vivien might find his half-dressed look and heavy breathing suggestive.

He entered the stairwell, and she grabbed him from behind around the neck the way he had grabbed her during the blackout. He turned around and kissed her. Her hands ran down his neck to the shirt collar, removing his tie.

"Do you want to take off my shirt too," he asked, "or should I unbutton it?"

"Hang on," she said, pulling the tie between her two hands as if she was testing the tensile strength of a garrote. "I'm new at this, so let's go slow."

"Whatever you want."

"I'm a little bit self-conscious too, so I'm going to put this tie on you like a blindfold." She covered his eyes with the tie, covering his ears also and tying it behind his head.

"You don't have any reason to be self-conscious, but if you are maybe you'd feel more comfortable in the privacy of my room…or yours, if you prefer."

"We can go to your room later," she said as she climbed the stairs, "but let's stay here for a few minutes. I've been thinking of the way you made me feel in here last time."

"Where did you go?" asked the Psycho, blindly reaching out for her. "You sound like you're higher than me now, but it's hard to tell with the echo and my ears covered."

"I'm up here," she said from the intermediate landing. "I'm laying here, waiting for you."

"Aren't you worried that someone will come in and catch us?"

"That's why I'm on the half landing," she answered. "If someone comes in from the floor above, we can go down. If someone comes in from down there, we can make our escape up. Besides, the thought of someone catching us kind of turns me on."

"You don't sound like someone who is self-conscious. Aren't you cold laying on the concrete floor?"

"Yes," she said, stepping over the body, "so come up here and help me get warm."

"Okay," said the Psycho, awkwardly groping for the stairs, "but it's a little tricky now that you've blindfolded me."

"I think you can manage."

"Do you mind if I take it off just until I get up there?"

"I wish you'd asked me a moment ago," she said. "Give me a sec to zip my jeans back up, and then you can take off your blindfold."

"No, no...that's okay—I found the railing. Stay just the way you are. I'm coming up."

"I can see that," she said, climbing halfway up the stairs past the intermediate landing. "I'm not the one who's blind-folded."

"You sound farther away again," the Psycho said as drew nearer to Vivian Sr.

"Sorry," she said, stretching out her neck so that her voice would project downwards. "My sweater was momentarily covering my face."

"That's not a problem," said the Psycho as he made the landing and touched one of the dead man's shoes. "Let me help you pull these off."

She watched for a moment from above as the Psycho struggled with the shoes; he seemed rather pitiful, blindfolded as he was and pawing at a corpse. "Now I want you to grab me around the neck…as hard as you can." Then she quietly slipped out into the hallway, signaling her roommate at the other end of the hall to pull the fire alarm.

As the alarm blared clamorously, Vivian and Vivien raced back towards their dorm room from opposite ends of the hallway, each pounding on the doors of their floor mates as they ran past them. They reached their room at the same moment, swiftly entering and closing the door behind them without slamming it shut. They sat on his bed, holding one another again. The sounds of their floor mates' commotion soon filled the hallway, most of them asking: is there really a fire? Someone answered that if there was, it was probably started by the freshmen on the top floor. Someone else volunteered to check the stairwell for smoke. Then they heard just what they'd hoped to hear, the staticky crackle of a voice transmitted through a walkie-talkie.

"Good," he said, "the Prodigy's still on the floor."

"They'll exit down the stairs," she said, "along with everybody else."

The next sound they heard was a bloodcurdling scream.

Chapter Twenty-nine

Vivien and Vivian sat conspiratorially close together at a table by themselves in the dining hall. It was Thursday night, and many of the students had already left for far-off spring break destinations, but those who remained observed the pair with a circumspect curiosity, or at least that's how it seemed to them.

"How did your appointment at the campus station go?" asked Vivien.

"The police told me they're considering it a crime of opportunity," answered Vivian, "given the Psycho's background."

"Background…as in arrest record?"

"As in student file," he answered, "replete with a preponderance of damning psychological evaluations that they assured me would all but guarantee a conviction. One of the detectives even insinuated that I'd have a good case if I decided to bring suit against the university."

"I still don't see why they'd think it was a crime of opportunity. His room was close enough to the ground floor that he probably took the stairs frequently. He must've passed other people all the time without murdering them."

"As you may recall," Vivian whispered, "he didn't actually murder my father. But the detectives conjectured that my dad likely looked out of place and possibly appeared confused and feeble due to his condition, so the Psycho may've seen him as an easy target. They also discovered marks on my dad's neck consistent with strangulation, and the Psycho was found holding a tie. You didn't try to choke my father, did you?"

"Of course not."

"Right, because that'd be crazy. Also, my father's shoes had been removed and neatly placed on the step below him… they didn't really have an explanation for that."

"One thing I hadn't considered until now was that since your dad…I mean the body," she said in a tone that to her ear sounded very close to sensitive, "was found on the half landing above the Psycho's floor, they must've thought he needed a motive to be on our floor and then to push the body down from there."

"They didn't mention that at all," he said. "Really it just seemed like they were relieved to have somebody like the Psycho behind bars. Between his file and the accounts given to them by the Prodigy's security detail, they see it as a pretty open and shut case. They told me he hasn't confessed yet, but they also told me he wasn't denying that he did it either."

"He didn't mention me at all?" she asked.

"Apparently not…maybe he knows how it looks and doesn't see the point in trying to convince them otherwise."

"Or maybe he's so in love that he'd rather go to jail than implicate me."

"Someone thinks quite a lot of her feminine charms, and I don't think the Psycho is capable of that type of selfless love, but you might be onto something…either way though, an innocent person is going to spend a very long time in prison."

"Innocent?" she asked under her breath. "That's not a word I ever thought you'd use to describe the Psycho. We all knew it was only a matter of time until he did something like this. What we did may have actually saved lives. Besides, I thought you hated the guy."

"I did...I do...I don't know. It just feels wrong. I mean according to doctors familiar with my brand of emotional hypersensitivity, I was in the highest risk category for committing suicide before my eighteenth birthday, and I'm still here."

Vivien used her fork to poke at some sort of casserole she had yet to taste. "I don't even know what this is."

"Me neither...why did you take it?"

"I thought I should put something on my plate, but I haven't had much of an appetite the past couple of days."

"The past couple of days?" he asked in disbelief. "I haven't been able to eat anything since Saturday."

"That's unfortunate. You must've gotten the same stomach bug as me a few days earlier. I hope it clears up for both of us by next week."

"I don't think it's a virus that has my gut in knots," he said. "What's so important about next week?"

"Spring break...our road trip."

"You still want to do that?" he asked incredulously.

"Sure, don't you?"

"I suppose it would look suspicious if we didn't go someplace."

"Good," she said. "Should we leave tomorrow then after your classes? I also have a meeting with my thesis advisor. I guess I'll need to tell him that I wasn't able to interview your dad. You don't think he'll make me pick someone else to write about, do you?"

"No, wait," he answered. "I forgot I promised my dentist that I'd make my Saturday morning appointment this time, so we can leave after that."

"You've canceled that appointment every week since you've been here," she said. "Why are you finally deciding to go over spring break?"

"Because I told him I would. He seemed pretty upset on the phone, and I just can't bear to let anybody else down."

Chapter Thirty

Vivien's Friday had been busier than she was accustomed to. She felt an impulse to attend all of her classes that day, even though in each of them most of the desks were vacant. The professor of her musicology course surveyed the two hundred or so empty seats of the lecture hall as he took the stage and then called over his six teaching assistants who acted as instructors for the weekly small group sections in which students were encouraged to ask questions about his lectures. The professor conferred in private on the far corner of the stage with his TAs, and then announced with magnanimity to the dozen or so students present that the TAs would take attendance and give extra credit to all those who came. With that he waved, wished everyone a mellifluent spring break, and exited stage left. Vivien was pleased with her good fortune, though she had some difficulty identifying the TA who led her section.

The meeting with her thesis advisor did not end on such a propitious note. The professor had read of Vivian Sr. in the campus newspaper. He asked her to convey his sympathies to her roommate and then inquired if she had thought of anyone else to write about. Vivien was taken aback. She had given her thesis almost no thought since the death of her roommate's father a week ago, which was only slightly less thought than she previously gave it, and she certainly hadn't considered starting anew and writing about someone else.

When she objected, the professor asked if she had been able to conduct her interview before the untimely passing of her thesis subject. She answered that she had not and quickly realized her mistake. She countered that the interview would have only offered the subject's limited perspective of himself; however, interviewing others who knew him would allow for a more complete portrait of the deceased alumnus. The professor agreed with her, and then asked who she knew that was close to Vivian Sr. that she could interview. She replied that she knew his son, of course, but was disinclined to interview him given the ghastliness of the circumstances surrounding his father's death. Then she remembered a mention of an old boxing buddy...Bob, perhaps?

The professor told her she needed to choose another thesis topic but that she shouldn't be concerned about the end of semester deadline. He could talk to his department head about an extension, and she would even be permitted to participate in the upcoming graduation ceremony, which she had no intention of attending; however, she wouldn't receive her diploma until her thesis was completed and approved. This was cause for concern. She could only just muster the effort to write a barely passable thesis while she was in school. The desultory prospect of trying to write one away from the structure of her campus life, such as it was, seemed absolutely impossible.

As she exited the dorm's elevator onto her floor, all she could think of was how nice it would be to collapse on her bed, then have a quiet dinner with Vivian at the cafeteria's last meal service before the break and finalize their vacation plans. When she turned the corner into the empty hallway, she could just make out her roommate's voice in their dorm room coming from the answering machine. Suddenly she had a sinking sensation in her gut that maybe they'd already had their last meal together. She scrabbled for her door key as she ran to the room. Finding the correct key, she stabbed it into the keyhole with enough force to grind the key's cuts against the lock's pins, and then hastily unlocked and flung the door open in an uninterrupted motion. She leapt across the room and grabbed the handset just as the line went dead.

She dropped the handset back in the cradle and waited for the microcassette to rewind. She pressed the button beneath the blinking light. "Vivian, don't wait for me to have dinner. I've got some errands to run tonight before our trip tomorrow, and besides I still don't have much of an appetite."

A long silence followed, she thought perhaps he'd quietly hung up or that the tape had stopped recording, but then she heard the honk of a car horn. "Sorry, I was just thinking of my father...what he told you about not wanting me to live in his shadow. I think he was right. I no longer have the fear of a child. For the first time in my life I feel like an adult...nothing frightens me anymore. Anyway, I should go. I'll see you soon."

She crawled into his bed and with tremulous hands wrapped herself tightly in sheets that were redolent of his expensive shampoo and his cheap shaving cream. She began to cry, only a little at first, but soon her face was streaked by tears whose briny taste was unfamiliar to her. What she hated most about her newly learned ability to read people was that she couldn't turn it off.

Chapter Thirty-one

Vivien hadn't so much slept through the night as she had denied her mind consciousness. Finally her eyes opened sometime in the midmorning. She looked around the room to confirm that she was still alone, which wasn't a surprise to her, but it brought on a new wave of sadness nonetheless.

She pulled the sheets to her neck and lay motionless, listening for sounds from the hallway. Soon security would make their final rounds, knocking on doors and announcing loudly before they moved onto the next floor that everyone must leave the building before it was locked down.

Unexpectedly, the silence was disrupted by the ringing of the telephone. She was sure it could be heard by anyone else on the otherwise unoccupied floor, but she continued to let it ring, questioning between the rings if she should allow herself to hope that it was him. Then she sprang from the bed and snatched the handset before the phone could ring a fifth time, not because she believed that it might be Vivian calling, but because she hadn't saved his message from the night before and was afraid a new message might record over it.

"Hello," she gasped into the mouthpiece.

"This is Doctor Odous. I'm calling for Vivian."

"He's not here. I'm his roommate."

"Please tell your roommate that my patience is at an end. He's missed his appointment for the umpteenth time this morning, despite giving me his word that he would be in today."

"He doesn't need a dentist—don't call here again."

She hung up the phone. Sitting at her desk, she looked at the empty street below, usually so filled with slow-moving cars and inattentive jaywalkers. Her mind drifted from what might've happened to Vivian Jr. to what had happened with Vivian Sr. She hadn't told her roommate that his father didn't die from the first impact, but rather was merely knocked insensible. She had stood him up again, thinking she would push him from the half landing to the floor below, but then realized from the traces of blood on the concrete floor it would be clear to investigators that there had been an impact on the intermediate landing and such a change in trajectory would remove all possibility of the fall being misconstrued as an accident, so she pulled him up as many steps as she could manage and pushed him once more, holding him momentarily at the waist so that his upper body pitched forward. Before she let him go, she had instructed him, "If you can still hear me, try landing head first this time so we can get this over with."

When his head hit the landing the second time she had heard his skull crack, but still he was not quite dead. He let out a last breath. She put her ear close to his mouth to hear any final words he might have to say, but there was only the sound of air leaving his lungs. His neck twisted slightly as his muscles lost tension. Inertia took hold of him, his body never again to move under its own power. She took what she thought would be one last look at the man she had killed, the father of the man she loved, and then climbed the stairs, noticing to her chagrin two different sets of scuff marks from his dress shoes.

She continued to scan the street, wondering where Vivian was, if he was still breathing, if he had anything to say.

Chapter Thirty-two

Vivien's spring break came to an end on Friday. The campus police, responding on Tuesday to a report of an abandoned vehicle on the top floor of a parking garage, discovered Vivian's body behind a lilac bush at the base of the eight-story structure. His skull was shattered so completely that his face had lost all form, making him unidentifiable by searching through student ID photos. It took 48 hours to determine his identity by his fingerprints. Wanting to inform his roommate of the situation, the police notified Vivian's erstwhile roommate, who explained that they had a falling out over flatulence the first week of the semester and that he had moved in with a female senior who shared the same name. Finding no emergency contact information for Vivien, and assuming she had left for parts unknown during the break week, they found her parents' phone number on her college application in her student file. Her father told the police that they hadn't seen Vivien since she left for college four years ago and had no earthly idea where she was. The police, not wanting Vivien to return to an empty dorm room and worry about her roommate's whereabouts, had a member of the dorm's security staff open the building and unlock her door so that they could leave a note for her to call the police station regarding her roommate. They found Vivien semi-conscious and half-starved. She hadn't stockpiled provisions, but she never left her room to forage for food in the off chance that Vivian might somehow return or phone.

The campus police reunited Vivien with her parents. Her father was elated to see his daughter again; the mother less so, as she had written off Vivien after a freshman year filled with unreturned phone calls, deciding instead to focus on her younger children. For Vivien's part, she longed for her campus cocoon and returned just three days into her sojourn at the family home under the pretext of needing to prepare for midterms.

She spent the remainder of the week following spring break sleeping in Vivian's bed and sneaking up food from the cafeteria. She left the residence hall for the first time on Friday to meet with her thesis advisor. She knocked on the professor's door. The professor sounded startled when he asked, "Vivien is that you?"

"Yes, professor." She could hear him approaching the other side of the door.

"It's a pleasure to see you dear," he said, as he opened the door and motioned for her to enter. "I wasn't expecting you, but I'm glad you're here. Please have a seat."

"Thank you." She sat down and watched the professor take his chair behind the desk.

"What can I do for you?" he asked, his cheery tone not correlating with the concern in his eyes.

"Well, I had a rather trying spring break—"

"Yes, I know dear," said the professor in a consolatory voice with his hands clasped. "I was saddened to hear of your roommate...I'm so sorry for your loss."

"Thank you...so I didn't have much of a chance to think of a new thesis topic, but perhaps we could brainstorm some ideas together."

"Vivien…have you not spoken with your dean yet?" the professor asked.

"She called and left a message, but I haven't been in to meet with her yet."

"I see…then this may come as a surprise to you, hopefully a pleasant one as you could undoubtedly use some good news now, but the administration has decided, given recent events, that you shall be awarded passing grades for all your courses this term, and thus, since this was to be your final semester, you have completed your degree. Congratulations, you've graduated."

"So I don't have to write a thesis?" she asked with a face full of frowns.

"No…your dean inquired as to how much of your thesis you had completed. I gave her a vague answer regarding the number of pages you'd written but assured her that you'd done a fair amount of research."

"But I haven't done any research," she said. "I didn't even have a thesis topic last time we spoke."

"Through no fault of your own. Let's just say I knew your heart was never in this project, and so I may have overstated the work you'd done in order to give you the benefit of the doubt."

"But I doubt I deserve any benefit."

"I thought you'd be pleased," the professor said with dismay. "You've shown great poise and courage throughout this ordeal…you've earned this."

"I don't feel as if I have."

"Do you know that Babe Ruth, arguably the greatest baseball player ever, holds the World Series record for strikeouts?"

"What does that have to do with me?" she asked with exasperation. "What should I do now?"

"We professors are the impoverished nobility of a failed nation, so maybe my advice shouldn't count for much, but take it from an old sinecurist like me—don't stay in any one place for too long."

PART TWO: THE MIDDLE WAY

Chapter One

Waiting room. An appellation as apt as it is austere. A dining room evokes thoughts of holiday feasting, while a living room brings to mind memories of friends and family; even a bathroom suggests cleansing ablutions, and a restroom offers relief and respite. However, a waiting room is perhaps the most accurately named room of all. Good news can be hoped for or anticipated anywhere, but when we wait for bad news it is best to do so in a waiting room.

I'm not waiting in a hospital for a prognosis. I'm waiting in an office building to interview for a job I don't want—a job I would've been embarrassed to take ten years ago—but today it's a job I need if I am to continue calling myself a working writer... there is no good news to be had here, only varying degrees of bad. I admire people who can make career changes in their forties. I can't even imagine what it must be like to go to an office every day...to have a boss who makes demands on your time and dictates your schedule. And those are the lucky ones. What if it turns out that my twenty years of writing experience are worthless? What if in the next chapter of my life I'm destined to play the role of a waitress or a salesclerk? Am I even qualified for those jobs?

"Vivien Leigh," says the attractive, young woman behind the reception desk, "the managing editor will see you now—go right in."

I stand and pick up my leather-bound portfolio, which feels ancient. The managing editor is probably all of twenty-five and has read everything I've written, or at least everything he thinks he needs to, on his mobile phone. My shirt collar feels too tight, as if I'm being slowly choked by a languid assassin with very weak hands. The fabric of my jacket doesn't breathe and my back is sweaty.

I enter the editor's office and am pleased to find it occupied by a woman who's twenty years my senior. "You look surprised," she says as she takes her seat behind a tastefully appointed, glass top desk.

"I was expecting—"

"Someone younger."

"A man...who was also younger," I say as I sit down in front of what might've once been a ceiling.

"With all the turnover in the newspaper business, editors jumping ship for more viable industries, I can see why you might've thought I was younger...but why male?"

"Your receptionist," I answer. "She seems the type a man would hire to impress his buddies."

"Ah...she's my niece."

"I can see the resemblance."

"On my husband's side...niece-in-law, I suppose."

"My mistake again."

"Don't worry, it won't count against you" she says, opening a file on her desktop—an actual manila file on her actual desktop; her computer is nowhere in sight...color me impressed. "As for my advanced years...maybe if I was your age I'd consider a career change, but what am I going to do now...go work at a chain restaurant or a department store? I'd be completely lost and perfectly miserable. No, I'm staying right here until they shutter the doors...which could be any day now."

I like her, and now I really want this job.

"I don't think this job is right for you," she says as she flips through what appear to be samples of my writing. "The position is for a person on the street sort of writer. You seem like someone who wants to stay cooped up in a room, exploring your interior life."

"As you may know, I did a series of well-received movie reviews for the local entertainment section of a New York newspaper."

"Yes, I have a few of them here: 'Citizen Kan't Take It with You,' 'Sophie Should've Chosen Something Less Depressing,' and my favorite 'Birth of a Nation: Super Not Racist.'"

"That last one was intended to be a satirical indictment of film's checkered history. My old editor insisted on those sorts of titles for my reviews. He wanted to kindle interest for classic movies that he thought readers might otherwise think were boring."

"The titles are catchy, as is the writing. 'A story so lachrymose that you'd be forgiven for mistaking the imperfections of the degraded cellulose as the film weeping at its own projected image.'" She takes off her reading glasses and sets them on top of the sample she'd been reading.

"Thanks," I say, not sure if that's the right response.

"These are all old movies."

"Yes, there were a number of neglected nostalgia theaters, as my editor called them, which were foundering at the time, so he asked me to—"

"You never wrote any reviews for contemporary movies?"

"No, those were done by a different section of the newspaper," I answer, "different staff, different pecking order."

"So you never tried to get assigned a new movie based on the strength of your reviews for these old movies?"

"I was more interested in trying to drum up business for those overlooked theaters, though sadly their end was inevitable."

"So then you actually went to these theaters?" she asks purposely.

"Pardon," I say, pretending not to understand the question because I am loath to tell lies—even in an interview.

"These hoary, rundown movie theaters...you went to see these classic films there?"

"Well...they were located all over the five boroughs. Travel logistics being what they are in NYC—"

"So you only went to the theaters that were conveniently located?"

"As I'm sure you know, when writing film reviews, you're afforded very few opportunities to see the movies before they open...even the rereleases, and I'm a somewhat slower writer than most film critics who are accustomed to tight deadlines, so when I could I tried to see the films well in advance in order to write a more considered review befitting these treasures of cinema."

"That's what I figured," she tells me. "You never went to a single one of these theaters. You watched them at home on DVD."

"VHS mostly...how did you know?"

"I spent the first half of my career as an investigative journalist," she answers. "You develop a nose for bullshit."

"I'm sorry if my answers sounded deceptive," I say contritely. "Yes, I am something of a homebody, but I think you'll see from my writing that it is possible to engage readers without actually having to engage with readers."

"The quality of your writing is not in question," she says as she thumbs through a few more samples. "It's why you got this interview in the first place; however, I've been following your career for some time now, and it seems in the past decade you've been on something of a down-market slide, moving from city to city. This city has just two daily newspapers, and I'm afraid they only print our small paper out of habit."

"Well you see, my career choices are largely based on my fragile ego. I've been searching for a position with an organization in which I can be reasonably sure that I'm one of the hundred best writers on staff."

"While I enjoy your self-deprecating humor in your writing, it has no place in a job interview."

"No, of course not," I say, sitting up in my chair. "I'm just a bit nervous because I think this paper might be a good fit for me, and I'm ready to settle down and grow some roots."

"You've no reason to be nervous...as I said you've proven yourself to be a capable writer. You first came on my radar about two decades ago with that little book of yours...what was it called?"

"*Study House*," I answer.

"That's right...I read it, you know."

"I think I'm supposed to say, 'so you're the one.'"

"Don't be so modest," she says. "Weren't you poised to be one of the next big authors?"

"I did have a sort of flash-in-the-pan success that lasted about fifteen minutes."

"That's more than most people get, despite what Mister Warhol believed."

"Thanks," I say. "I'm glad you liked it."

"I said I read it; I didn't say I liked it," she corrects.

"Oh, I'm sorry you didn't like it."

"Don't be sorry, and I didn't say I didn't like it either. I thought it showed promise, but it was too much dialogue for me...felt like I was reading a movie script. Let's just say it wasn't my cup of tea."

"Sure, okay...I don't even like tea that much anyway." I have no idea whose voice is coming out of my mouth right now, but I'm fairly certain it isn't mine.

"So what happened?" she asks. "Why aren't you a novelist now?"

"Writing that story was cathartic for me…kind of an exercise, like a senior thesis of sorts, and the story was a simulacrum of my college experiences—"

"Simulacrum…remember, I'm just a simple newspaper gal here," she says.

"What I mean is the narrative wasn't so much based on events that really happened but rather my impression of being a college student in the nineties. So I think, for a brief time, it struck a chord."

"I should say so," she agrees. "I remember there was talk in the industry that your small, self-published eBook was a harbinger of the printed word's demise."

"Yeah, mine was part of an early wave of electronic novels and novellas that circulated via email. We gave away our eBooks to anyone who wanted to read them, not thinking that anybody really would."

"And how did that work out for you?" she asks with a knowing grin.

"Not great. Once we realized that people were actually reading our books, it was too late to monetize them since there were already so many digital copies floating around in cyberspace. I never intended to make any money off my novella, mind you, but it's a surreal experience to have someone ask for your autograph while you're standing in line for a free Thanksgiving turkey."

"So why didn't you go the traditional route and do a print edition?" she asks. "Did you think you'd lose cred among your disruptive little movement or were you just too proud?"

"Not at all, and it wasn't a movement exactly…only a group of us who wanted to share our stories. I was approached by a few publishers, but they each offered contracts that would've required me to expand on my story so there would be new content not found online. I tried to write more, but I just didn't have anything else to say about my college experience...I'd moved on."

"Then why not write about your new experiences afterwards?"

"I tried that too," I answer, "but the publishers weren't interested. They thought readers would only identify with what I'd written about college life, since the life I lived afterwards was more...singular...I believe is how the last publisher I was in contact with put it. Besides, my notoriety as one of the self-publishing pioneers or whatever had pretty much dissipated by then."

"Sure, nowadays every fool with a laptop is writing an eBook or a blog and nobody knows who to read anymore, so nobody reads much of anything. I imagine soon there'll be more writers in the world than readers."

"Maybe so," I say, thinking it's already happened, though I keep quiet as I imagine admitting so will hurt my chances for landing this writing job.

"Whatever happened to your roommate?" she asks. "I presume he didn't really commit suicide or that you didn't really push his father down a flight of stairs to his death."

"No, those were all composite characters—it wasn't a roman à clef. I never had a male roommate. I created him as sort of a yin to the yang of the protagonist, which is why I gave them similar names, and even though the protagonist had the same name as me, she was more like other girls I knew." I told you I am loath to tell lies; I didn't say I never do it.

"But you said yourself that you're a homebody...just like she was."

"Well, not to the same degree," I say. "I mean, I didn't hide in my dorm room over winter breaks or anything like that."

"But all art is autobiography in some way."

"Maybe, though I think I'm more like Patty if I had to pick one of the characters as an analogue for me."

"Speaking of words that sound similar to anal," she says, "I guess better her than that fellow obsessed with his bowel movements."

"Yes, I agree."

"So you never see the old gang?" she asks.

"Hardly ever."

"Not even at class reunions?"

"I don't think I'm the University's favorite alumnus, owing to some of the things I wrote about my college experience," I answer. "I imagine they'd prefer I didn't tell people I graduated from there...I'm not exactly on their mailing list."

"That's a pity, though I can see how if readers took your depiction of Study House too literally it would give the school a black eye."

"I never identified the school specifically, but certainly there have been those who've assumed that I was describing my alma mater."

"I think it'd be a hoot for your classmates to guess who they were in your story, since you never used full names, except for the two main characters, choosing nicknames instead for your supporting characters that were suggestive of case studies, though I suppose they might be cross that you gave them all mental disorders."

"Maybe," I say, "I imagine it's all water under the bridge by now."

"I'm sure they understood that by attributing mental disorders to each of your characters, you were commenting on how our society tends to see individuals with psychological issues as diagnoses rather than complete people who have both flaws and talents."

"I'm sure."

"That Prodigy character you described," she says, "he's not by chance the creator of the Flipped M School that everyone can't stop talking about these days, is he?"

"I don't...no—I don't know."

"But I see from your resume that you were at the same college at the same time as him, weren't you?"

"I'm not sure," I answer equivocally, "I mostly kept to myself, so even if we were there at the same time, I doubt our paths ever crossed, and if we did meet, I certainly don't remember him."

She leans back in her chair and looks upwards. Perhaps she's sniffing the air for more bullshit.

"So you really want this job?" she asks the acoustic tiles above us.

"I absolutely do."

"Okay, I know you've got the chops, let's see if you've got the stomach. I'll start you out as a contract writer. You'll get paid per column. I expect at least one column a week but no more than three in any seven days...for now."

"Great," I reply, "what sort of columns should I—"

"Think common man like Studs Terkel and city beat like Mike Royko," she says, "but make it your own."

"Make it my own...I can do that."

"Mix it up though," she continues, "sometimes funny, but never silly, and sometimes poignant, but never maudlin."

"Got it. One last question—"

"No, you don't have to come into the office," she answers my half-asked question. "You can just email me your stories."

"Thanks boss."

Chapter Two

Cream soda. I don't know why, but I really want one. I haven't had one in years…in fact, I can't recall ever drinking one at all, but I must've had one at some point because now I crave the very specific taste of it. Don't most people leave a job interview and head for the nearest bar? There are renowned taverns on almost every corner near the newspaper's office that once served some of the city's most esteemed writers, and here I am looking for a soda shop. At least it's a sunny afternoon to be outside and quite warm for January.

I told Patty I'd stop by after my interview to tell her how it went…at least this time I have good news to report. We've been friends ever since college, but these days I look forward to seeing her three-year-old son more than his mom. He's a beautiful little boy, and it's been over a decade since I've been on a date, so I think being his pretend auntie is as close as I'll ever get to being a mother myself.

The looming prospect of forty hit Patty pretty hard. She's as attractive now as she ever was, and though she had plenty of suitors, she never could decide on any one of them. Eventually even she could see the pattern. So just before her fortieth birthday, she made a deal with the devil, or the next worst thing—Digy, in order to have a baby. She would raise their child, and he could visit as much or as little as he wanted. No strings attached: no guilt, no commitment. She got her baby, and the Prodigy got his progeny.

Maybe not the worst bargain a woman approaching the end of her child-bearing years ever made to get pregnant—that came later. Soon after she told Digy she was expecting, she lost her job at the public relations agency she'd worked at for years when it was suddenly acquired and summarily dismantled by a holding company. Despite having a reputation in the industry as a creative mind that was always good for a new idea, she couldn't land another job. Phone calls and emails weren't returned by people who would send her Christmas cards. She knew the fix was in…we all knew it.

The only person who pretended not to know was the one who orchestrated it. Digy offered her an entire floor of one of his buildings, to be decorated however "she wished, in order" to cheer her up. She would never need to work again and never want for anything. The prospect of being a stay-at-home mom appealed to her, but of course there was a price. Their baby was to be an experiment of sorts, in much the same way his father had been, though the experiment would test a new hypothesis. The baby would not be taught to speak. Patty could hold him and hum to him, but she could not talk to him or sing songs to him. All guests would be vetted, pass through layers of security, and sign a contract that outlined the terms and conditions for visiting Patty and her child as well as the draconian penalties for noncompliance.

Patty was now a royal prisoner in a fortified palace, but she could come and go as often as she pleased, though usually not without a security detail. Her son, however, had to stay in the building, tended to by the most qualified and taciturn childcare professionals available, all under constant audio surveillance.

For his part, Digy was actually a doting father, despite never talking to his son. He had the building's helipad converted into a rooftop garden, to which only Patty's penthouse had access. He even took up semi-permanent residence on the floor below hers soon after their son was born.

As strange as their situation is, Patty and her son really do have everything. Everything but cream soda, I bet. Patty became something of a health nut in her thirties, and now she's one of those mothers who only gives her kid organic this and non-GMO that, as if the boy weren't insulated enough already. Maybe if find a convenience store that sells cream soda on my way, I'll buy two cans and smuggle one in for the kiddo.

Chapter Three

Lepidopterarium. That's where the security guard who let me in told me I could find Patty and her son. Apparently he's having his weekly lesson with a retired professor of entomology. I can't decide what's more absurd: a professor who teaches without using words, or a three-year old who has his own butterfly house.

I climb the stairs to the rooftop garden and spot Patty sitting alone on a bench near the perimeter safety fence just past the heated koi pond. "Where's the kiddo?"

"Oh, hello Vivien," she says, appearing to come out of a trance brought on by the hypnotic gurgling of the pond's fountain. "He's back there with the bug doctor and the nanny."

"You don't like sitting in on his butterfly lessons?"

"It's not that I mind, it's that I can't help but laugh, which is, as you know, verboten…or at least frowned upon."

"You find butterflies funny?" I ask.

"Not particularly, but a septuagenarian who spends an hour a week flapping his arms for a three-year old is hilarious."

"That does sound rather amusing," I say as I sit down beside her. She uncrosses her arms. Her heavy sweater feels soft as it brushes against my wrist.

"How did your interview go? Were you asked any of those silly questions like, 'What's the most creative way you would use a paperclip?'"

"Thankfully no," I say, "although my stock answer for that one is that I pretend the paperclip is the length of a football field, and I use it to help prop up the Leaning Tower of Pisa."

"That's creative…though it seems a little like cheating to imagine it as any size you want, but then it's a dumb question anyway."

"I've often wondered how many good hires haven't been made because applicants were misjudged under the unique and stressful circumstances of an interview," I say as the lowlight reel of my awkward interviews plays in my head.

"Uh oh…that sounds like it didn't go very well."

"At one point I did feel as if I'd regressed back to my teenage self, but it went well enough…I got the job."

"That's wonderful news," Patty says as she turns to hug me, but then thinks better of it, and instead warmly pats me on the back.

"Thanks," I say, trying hard not to recoil from her contact.

"We should celebrate!"

"Sure, do you have any wine," I ask, "or cream soda?"

"I have mineral water and and beet juice."

"No, I'm good."

"We can go to a pub," she offers.

"That's okay," I say. "I want to see the kiddo…besides it's a nice day to be outside, and this really might be the loveliest spot in the whole city."

"It's certainly the quietest," Patty replies. "I'm proud of you Vivien. I know you weren't excited about this job, but I'm sure you'll be great at it. I think you've become the most successful of us all."

"Not counting your son's father, of course…though I suppose he's always been playing a different game than the rest of us."

"Speaking of the rest of us," she segues, "I received an email from the Schiz the other day."

"I haven't seen him since Poopy's wake. How is he?" I ask, trying to sound genuinely interested.

"As you know, he took Poopy's death pretty hard…he doesn't handle loss well."

"He certainly doesn't handle funerals well," I say, thinking back to the scene the Schiz made in the funeral home's parking lot when he attempted to rend the lapel of his durably-constructed, polyester-blend suit jacket.

"I think Poopy's colon cancer—I suppose we shouldn't call him that now that he's dead—confirmed for the Schiz that we're all cursed by our disorders."

"Poopy wasn't cursed, and his fecal fixation wasn't his disorder, but rather a side-effect of his therapy," I say. "And he could've beaten the cancer if he hadn't refused treatment and allowed the doctors to cut out the malignant tumors in his large intestine."

"We don't know that for certain," Patty reproves. "But the good news is that the Schiz recently started taking an experimental medication that he said is helping with his akathisia, so it sounds like he's doing better. He's even back together with his wife."

"I didn't realize they'd separated."

"I've mentioned it a few times before."

"Sorry, I must've forgotten," I say, feeling something that approximates guilt. "I'm pleased for him. I hope it works out with his wife this time, and I also hope that his medication keeps him from talking to himself when he eats."

"You're wicked," Patty says with a gleam in her eye. "You know he hasn't talked to himself while chewing since our sophomore year."

"I guess I'd forgotten that as well. If you don't mind my saying, I've noticed that your condition seems to have improved too. I don't think you've had a personality transition the last several times I've seen you."

"Yeah," she agrees vaguely. "I have fewer decisions to make these days, so I'm less stressed, which is good since I want to be a source of stability in my son's life—not a patchwork parent."

"I'm sure any personality you might ever shift to would care for him just the same. Who knows…if your personality starts transitioning again, maybe he'd think of you as more mommy to love."

"While that's a pleasant notion," Patty says, "I'm in no hurry to test your theory."

"What theory is that?" Digy asks, approaching from the nearby rooftop entrance.

"That there's no such thing as privacy in this building," Patty says acerbically.

"Bosh, that's your theory my dear—not Vivien's. Besides, as is clearly evident, we are on this building and not 'in' it."

Though Digy is a frequent topic of conversation, both between Patty and myself as well as with the public at large, this is the first time I've seen him in person in almost two decades. He's filled out and lost the awkward angles and acned skin of youth, and though his face still looks young, his eyes have grown old. Patty has confided in me before that she thought Digy was growing more handsome with age while she was losing her looks, which is ridiculous; Patty is still a looker by anyone's reckoning, but I thought her estimation of Digy's increasing handsomeness was based on her anxiety about being in her forties while he was still in his thirties; however, seeing Digy now, I must agree that he is aging well…if only he'd stop using words like bosh.

"Hello Vivien," he says, standing next to the koi pond. "It's been some time."

"Yes, it has." He's waiting for me to say more, but there isn't anything else I wish to add, and I make it a policy not to talk when I have nothing to say.

"Your son is in the butterfly house," Patty says. "In case you were wondering why we were speaking out loud."

"I always know where my son is," he says pointedly. "So, Vivien, what brings you here today?"

"Vivien just got a new job," Patty answers for me, "and she's been telling me about her interview."

"I wish you'd told me you were looking for work," Digy says. "I could always use another writer on my staff."

"Oh, I couldn't work for you."

"And why's that?" he asks.

"I'd be afraid I might fall out of favor with the boss and lose my job."

"That's how employees usually lose their jobs," Digy says, "when their work doesn't meet with the approval of the boss."

"It's not my writing that I'd be worried wouldn't meet with approval," I reply, "and somehow I think you might have a way of making my unemployment a permanent condition."

"I think Patty's paranoia must be rubbing off on you," Digy responds. "Sincerely though, congratulations on your new position…wherever it may be. Your good news puts me in mind of the Schiz. Has my son's mother mentioned that she recently received an email from him?"

"He reads my emails and then wonders why I'm paranoid?"

"Tosh, the Schiz said he was going to email you to say that his life of late is much improved."

"He told you about the new medication he's on?" Patty asks with surprise and a hint of disappointment.

"Who do you think got him into the clinical trials for the medication?"

"That was decent of you to help the Schiz," I say, looking past Digy at the armed sentry now standing near the rooftop entrance. "What'd you have to do to get him in…lean on your government connections?"

Rather than answering, Digy offers a puzzled expression, and then looks over his shoulder at the guard. "Oh, he's not government issue. He's on my payroll to protect me from governments...ours and others."

"Now, who's being paranoid?" Patty asks.

"I wish my concerns were mere paranoia," Digy says with a solemnity that suggests an earned maturity, "but regrettably they are all too real."

"Why would the government be after you?" I ask. "Weren't you once their prized prodigy?"

"I was until we had a falling out over some ideas of mine," he says with a know-it-all smirk. There's the old Digy that I know and loathe. "Now our government wants to discredit me; it's other entities that seek to do worse. I have no doubt that I'm being surveilled now—out in the open as we are. I must tell you that it's quite refreshing to talk with someone who hasn't committed my curriculum vitae to memory and hasn't read at length about the peculiarities of my entrepreneurial endeavors."

"I've seen your name in the headlines over the years," I say, "but I never read much further than that."

"Vivien has chosen to focus on her interior life these days," Patty explains, which I suppose is true, but I hadn't realized she was aware of it or that it was considered a conscious choice on my part.

"Haven't you spent most of your career as a freelance writer?" Digy asks. "Often writing for newspapers?"

"You don't have to read them to write for them," I answer.

"Fascinating," Digy says. "I've followed your writing career somewhat over the years, so I suppose I've read more of your articles than you've read of mine."

"Perhaps," I reply, "but then mine are by me and not about me."

"True," he says, "though all art is autobiography in some way."

"You're the second person who's told me that today," I reply. "I agree that it is, though I don't agree that's what I do... at least not of late."

"Your novella then," Digy says, "the one about our time together in college—wasn't that art imitating life, or do I have that backwards?"

"I'm not sure," I answer. "Frankly, I'm surprised you read it."

"I didn't read it from cover to cover," he says, "but the gist of it was relayed to me."

"Well, it was an eBook, so it didn't have covers," I reply, trying to keep my voice steady to mask my annoyance. "How long would it have taken someone who reads as fast as you to finish it?"

"To read it would've interfered with my work," he says, "like a major league baseball player swinging a Wiffle Ball bat, but let's get back to what we were discussing."

"What we were discussing was your falling out with the government," I say.

"But discussions so often seem to center around me, whether I want them to or not," he says. "For a change of pace, why don't you answer some of my questions, and then I'll answer some of yours? You know, like a normal conversation."

"Fine," I reply.

Patty turns away from me slightly on the bench. It's a subtle shift, but I wonder if it's indicative of a personality transition.

"Since you didn't use your roommate's real name, and there was no record of him transferring to your dorm room, the University had no official reason to investigate the accounts described in your story, despite their similarity to events that actually occurred, including the death of a student living in—and I particularly liked what you called our dormitory—Study House."

"You haven't asked a question," I say.

"I never ask questions I already know the answers to," he replies. "It's one of my flaws."

"So the question you already know the answer to is…"

"Did you kill your roommate's father?" Patty asks with a strained voice that I've never heard her use. "I guess we never really talked about that before."

"Why don't you ask the guy with all the answers?" I suggest, irritated by what feels like my second interrogation of the day.

"Come now," Digy says, "there's no need for a defensive tone. You're among old friends."

"Old friends who want to know if I'm a murderer."

"I wouldn't say that Patty wants to know, and I already do know. My security team investigated the incident just after it happened and concluded that the Psycho likely wasn't the perpetrator, but since he was on their watch list, it was fine with them that a potential threat was incarcerated. So when the University asked my team, unofficially of course, whether they thought it was a valid arrest, they responded that it was, which was good enough for the school."

"So you assume that if it wasn't him then it must've been me?"

"I don't assume anything," he answers, "and moreover I don't care."

"Then why did you bring it up?" I ask.

"To warn you. As he was with my previous security team, the Psycho is on my current team's naughty list, and he's due to be released from prison next month. I suspect that two decades of incarceration have not made him any nicer."

Not wanting to meet Digy's gaze, and unsure of where to look, I stare up at the sky. Three cumulus clouds appear to be converging into one tumid mass, blocking the sun with their union.

Patty is the first to break the silence; her voice no longer sounds strained. "I interpreted your character's confession as taking responsibility for the guilt we all shared, our characters that is, for not taking better care of one another, since we all knew that each of us was damaged in some way, and we also knew how isolating that felt, but instead we pretended that we weren't afflicted and ignored the suffering of others, and so...to a degree... we were all complicit in both the murder and the suicide."

"Sweet Patty," says Digy with more condescension than one might think could fit into two little words, "another few steps in that direction and I fear you'll turn yourself in for kidnapping the Lindberg baby."

"Speaking of guilty," I say, wanting to give Patty a break, "what got the government upset with you? I thought you did just what they wanted by teaching the entire world to speak English, or at least your dumbed-down version of it."

"You're too generous," he says. "That online course I created has so far only helped a little more than a billion people to speak and read simplEng, but then who's counting?"

"I imagine there are many people who are counting," I answer, "in fact the last tally I saw calculated that simplEng is now the dominant language on the planet. Opening up markets around the globe, positioning English-speaking countries to spread their views and agendas through commerce."

"Why Vivien, you've developed a liberal streak, and all this time I thought you didn't care about anything or anyone," Digy digs. "You make selling bubblegum and tube socks sound diabolical."

"Diabolical ...no," I say, "deceptive, duplicitous, devious, disingenuous, and deleterious...probably."

"You forgot dishonest and deceitful, but are we still talking about strategies for global domination or me?" Digy asks with feigned indignation.

"Well, you still haven't answered my question…and I know how you never forget a question."

"Too true," he agrees, though I wasn't sure if he was agreeing about not having answered my question or never forgetting a question. "They'll say that it wasn't, but it was my idea to teach the simpler version of the English language I'd developed via an online course. All it required was a slight acceleration of technological progress in underserved markets— mostly mobile broadband penetration. You should've heard some of the ridiculous ideas bandied about before then: having military aircraft drop *McGuffey Readers* tucked inside of Sears and Roebuck catalogs over Third-World countries."

Patty shifts again on the bench next to me but remains silent.

"So after some fits and starts, we get the whole program up and running, and it exceeds all expectations. People in places you've never heard of learn our language on second-hand cell phones and gray-market tablets, and the first thing they want to do with their newfound knowledge is shop. They want to wear what we wear, watch what we watch, and eat what we eat."

"Or at least what the corporations who manufacture those fungible commodities tell them we wear, watch, and eat," I say.

"Precisely, the goal was never to teach a language but rather to teach a culture, and I'm cognizant of how that sounds, but there is charity that accompanies the commerce. As our world gets smaller and more interconnected, we take notice of people who have heretofore gone unnoticed, and they take notice of us, for better and for worse. Citizens of affluent countries are more likely to give to people living on the other side of the globe if they feel a kinship with them, perhaps through shared music or movie preferences. Likewise, residents of the most impoverished parts of the planet are less likely to feel antipathy towards us if they see that we have a predilection for the same salty snacks and athletic apparel as they do. Statistically, a terrorist is 53 percent less likely to blow up people who wear similar sneakers."

"That sounds like a made up statistic," I accuse.

"Maybe, but that doesn't mean it isn't true."

"Now should come the part when you explain what precipitated the falling out," I push.

"Ah, yes. Well my little simplEng course was such a success that I thought: why not make more of them?"

"Why not indeed," Patty chimes in.

"So I started my own company," Digy continues, "which our government opposed. I hired the best minds money could rent to develop online courses, which our government opposed. Now my free college courses—"

"Free from tuition, not free from advertising," I clarify, "that your company is paid handsomely for, I imagine."

"Correct," he says. "See, you know more about me than you let on. In the last few years, my humble online institution of higher learning—"

"The Flipped M School, which serves…I mean educates…millions," I say.

"Has become so disruptive to traditional education that many longstanding brick-and-mortar universities are now moribund due to shrinking enrollment."

"Which our government opposes," I add. "I wonder what our alma mater thinks of its most famous alumnus now."

"You and Patty are alumni. I never actually graduated, though I did accept an honorary doctorate some years ago."

We hear footsteps on the gravel path and turn to see one of the nannies walking toward us. She carries a paddle sign at her side and appears eager to make a report. "Your son is finishing up his lesson and will be joining you momentarily."

"Good, I was hoping for a chance to say 'hello,'" I quip.

"You do and you'll never see him again," Digy threatens.

"Has he started talking yet of his own volition?" I ask Patty.

"He's making sounds, but he seems confused by them," she answers with maternal concern.

"How much longer can you go without talking to him?" I ask.

"As long as it takes," Digy answers. "He will teach us his language, which he'll invent for himself...humankind's first unalloyed, not ad hoc language created free of committee. I hope his first word will be the name he chooses for himself."

"If you let him pick his own name, it's going to sound like he was named by a caveman," I hypothesize.

The nanny standing near us gets a signal in her earpiece and excitedly holds up the golf sign above her head that reads: QUIET PLEASE.

Soon the little boy appears on the path, followed by another nanny and the professor. When he sees his father, he breaks into a clumsy-cute run, nearly toppling Digy over as he hugs his father's kneecaps together. He's as beautiful as his mother. I tousle his hair with one hand and wave down to him with the other.

Chapter Four

L? Or is it El—I ruminate as I ride the elevated train back to my home, which is located in a pocket of the city that's midway between post-slum and pre-gentrified, depending on who you ask and what they're selling. El for elevated seems right, but then would that be confusing for the many Spanish speakers in this city who would read it as the the train? Besides, if you're going to shorten a word, wouldn't it make more sense to abbreviate it to only one letter rather than two?

The train clacks as riders yak…not to each other but on their cell phones. We lurch to a stop as the train pulls into a station. I am almost as far from the heart of the city where Patty lives as one can be and still be within the city proper. When I boarded the train, all the cars were crowded with commuters, but as we near the end of the line there are plenty of seats to be had, with a few thug-looking types lounging menacingly, each sprawled across several seats. The station announcements sound louder out here, and I used to think they turned up the volume to distract from the vicissitudes of the neighborhoods the train passes through, but I've come to learn that it's a trick of the ear—fewer riders to absorb the squawks from the p.a. system.

Mine is the next stop. I live in an unfinished condo building not too far from the station. The only question I had for the realtor who sold me the unit was about the projected occupancy when the building was completed. He told me what he thought I wanted to hear, saying that the building would be finished before the summer, and then the units would be snatched up at prices much higher than I, the condo's first resident, would pay. Unfortunately for the developers, the building has suffered a number of setbacks that have brought progress to a near standstill. Lately it's been a rash of mysterious frozen pipes. It seems someone has been opening water lines to a trickle in unheated parts of the basement, and the pipes quickly freeze and burst in the harsh winter nights. Despite not knowing how the vandals gain access to the building or recalling such pernicious vandalism at any of their other sites, the management team assures me that the building is secure. I believe them. The frequent fluctuations of water pressure as they repair the pipes notwithstanding, I enjoy the peace and quiet of my very own condominium building.

The train arrives at my stop and the doors slide open. I get off. As I begin to descend the stairs from the platform to the street below, I catch a glimpse of one of the thugs slithering between the closing train doors. I try to quicken my pace down the steps, but an old lady with a collapsible shopping cart laden with groceries occludes the narrow stairway opening. I help the lady get the cart onto the sidewalk. The thug pushes past, almost knocking my portfolio out from under my arm, and hurries away. Maybe I'm as paranoid as Patty and Digy.

The lady waves and mumbles a thank you as she pulls her big coat tight against the gusting wind. It had been a lovely afternoon on the rooftop garden, but now that the sun has gone down and the wind has picked up, the temperature has dropped precipitously. The ungloved lady continues to hold her zipper-less coat closed as she pushes her groceries in the opposite direction I'm going. I wrap my scarf around my neck and head toward home. As I round the corner, I spot a small, smoldering ember in a darkened doorway. The thug from the train is smoking and staring at me.

I keep walking. He flicks his cigarette into the street and starts to follow. I must've stood out on the train in my interview clothes. My condo is only half a block up. The street is deserted; the only sound is the howl of the wind and the rustle of blowing paper on the sidewalk. I walk faster to test him, and I can see over my shoulder that he matches my pace. I make it to the entrance of my building and take my time typing in the security code on the keypad. There's no way I can get inside and shut the door behind me, with the resistance from its heavy-duty pneumatic closer, before the thug could reach me if he decides to break into a sprint. He tries to look nonchalant as he approaches, not making eye contact as I pull open the door and watch him through the glass, gauging his height.

I enter my building and quickly climb the stairway to the first floor, with the top step making its familiar creak. One would think that a new construction wouldn't have creaky stairs. As I turn the corner into the dimly lit hallway, I hear him tentatively climb the stairs, pausing briefly halfway between the ground floor and where I'm standing. Most of me hopes he reconsiders and turns around. He doesn't and recommences his ascent. I put down my portfolio and pick up the baseball bat that I always leave leaning in the doorjamb of the first unit when I go out. I can hear him struggling to breathe as he nears. It's one flight of stairs—how much does this guy smoke? The creak announces his arrival at the top step. I raise the bat. Although I can't see him, I know he's just around the corner. This must be how a baseball player feels when he tries to hit an elusive pitch that's thrown too fast to track—that makes me think of Digy's comment about swinging a Wiffle Ball bat. If only my old thesis advisor could see me now. There are too many thoughts in my head, and I'm distracting myself...I need to focus; this situation requires my undivided attention. I swing the bat hard and make solid contact. It feels like I hit a homerun as I hear the bridge of his nose crack. He falls backwards down the stairs, tumbling end over end.

I watch as he hits the ground floor headfirst. I hope I haven't killed him; I wouldn't know what to do with the body, as this condominium's modern furnace won't work for cremation. As the only occupant of a secured building, I think I'd be the primary suspect for murdering the dead guy at the bottom of the stairs, but then I could always claim self-defense, which is mostly true. He's young though, and in addition to having bad lungs, he's probably got a thick skull. The crumpled mass that is my aspirant assailant begins to stir. He raises up to his knees, using one hand to cover his spurting nose and the other to steady himself against the door.

"The police are on their way," I call down to him, staying back in the shadows of the hallway so he can't get a good look at me, though I can tell he sees the barrel of the bat real well. He gets his feet under him, pushes the door open, and slinks out into the night.

From what I can see, there's some bloody tile down on the landing...maybe a palm print on the door. I'll clean it up later on my way to the basement after I've gotten my wrench. It's been a busy day, and all I want to do now is listen to the answering machine. Most days I play a digital recording of his last message on my computer, but tonight I think I'll treat myself and plug in the old machine. The sounds on the cassette are so distorted now that I can't make out the words anymore, but of course I know them by heart, and I like the way his voice on the tape ages with mine. I carry my portfolio and my bat down the long hallway toward home.

Chapter Five

Plexiglas. I don't miss talking to the Psycho through it. When I used to visit him at the maximum security prison during his first decade of incarceration, we sat directly across from each other and spoke into heavy, pay-phone-style handsets through Plexiglas—the reflection of my face transposed onto his. Now that he's been transferred to a medium security facility—for good behavior, of all things—prisoners and their visitors can sit together at small tables. He still prefers for me to call him the Psycho rather than his actual name; he says it reminds him of better times, if you can believe that.

After each of the visitors has signed in and been cleared through the security center, we are made to wait outside the locked visiting room. The small corridor connecting the security center to the visiting room fills up fast as visitors file in from the security line. I've never understood why they make us wait here. The visiting room has 64 small tables. The busiest times of the year are around Christmas and Father's Day. Last month there were forty or so people waiting, which is by far the most visitors I've ever seen here at once, and they still made us wait in this corridor, despite the fact that there are plenty of tables to sit at in the visiting room and plenty of spaces to stand in the security center. Lately I've taken to staying in my rental car until the last possible moment before I enter the security center so that I can be last in line and thus wait in the corridor for the least amount of time with the amassed, unwashed masses.

After three different prison guards count us, they open the door to the brightly lit visiting room. The first-time visitors always rush to claim an open table, not realizing that there are more than enough. Once everyone is seated, they begin releasing the inmates from the locked door on the other side of the room one at a time, only to be called back in that same order an hour later. The third prisoner to enter the visiting room is #6655321. His eyes light up as he spots me seated at one of the middle tables of the last row. I like to sit as far away as possible so that I have more time to assess him as he walks towards me. At his old prison he often looked malnourished, and he would sometimes walk with a hitch in his step. Since he's been transferred here, his weight has appeared consistently healthy and his gait fluid.

When he reaches the eighth row of tables he turns in my direction, and I stand to give him a brief hug. I am pleased that his face is absent of bruises and his eyes are clear. We sit close enough to hold hands above the table, which is permitted, but we don't; I've come a long way with my personal contact issues over the years, but not quite that far. Instead I lightly rub the sleeve of his coarse jumpsuit.

"You know, you don't have to keep visiting me every month. They're going to let me out soon."

"I'd visit you every week if the drive wasn't so far."

"You make it sound as if your social life is almost as non-existent as mine," he says with regret, though I can't tell if it's for me or him. "Did you get that job you wrote me about?"

"I did."

"I knew you would."

"I tell you about every interview I have and most of them don't work out. How did you know I'd get this one?"

"I figure you deserve any job you want, and I'm always astonished when you don't get an offer…it's positively criminal; those hiring managers should be locked up in—"

"Okay that's enough," I say. "You know I have a low threshold for flattery."

"It's only part flattery. With my impending release date fast upon me, your struggles to find a job make me anxious about my prospects for gainful employment."

"I have something of a checkered résumé working against me."

"More checkered than this place?" he asks.

I take in the familiar grid of square tables and shrug. "I could still confess and get your record expunged. From what I understand the wrongly convicted often do rather well for themselves, and I'm not exactly making the most of my life anyway."

"Keep your voice down," he whispers as a prison guard walks past our table. "I don't want them to hear you talk like that."

"So where are you going to stay when you get out?" I ask. "As I've mentioned before, there are plenty of empty units in my building."

"I'm fairly sure squatting would be considered a violation of my parole. Besides, they've assigned me to live for at least a few months at a halfway house."

"I've never seen people living in half a house," I say. "Maybe I could stop by for dinner some evening."

"I think they keep it locked down pretty tight at night and from what I understand the food's lousy."

"Sounds like our old dormitory…actually this place reminds me a little of Study House too."

"Does it?" he asks, viewing the the cinderblock walls and fluorescent lights with a new perspective. "They take a firmer stance on loud music, but the rooms are about the same size."

"Speaking of our old dorm life, I saw Patty the other day."

"How's her son," he asks, "still a mime?"

"Mute and cute as ever," I answer. "I saw Digy too. I hadn't seen him since our college days, unless, of course, you count almost every time I turn on the news."

"A bunch of guys in here are taking those Flipped M courses of his. They that say once you get used to the simplEng the courses are really easy. Even some of those that never graduated from high school have earned college degrees."

"Sure, it's easy to earn a degree when you don't actually learn anything."

"I wouldn't be so sure," he says. "A few of the guys have earned their Juris Doctorates. Their degrees may not be ABA-accredited, but they learned enough to handle their own appeals, and one ex-con from here is now a practicing attorney in Louisiana."

"Does he practice spelling too whenever he needs to write the word witness: flipped em-I-T-N-E-S-S?" I ask facetiously. "Or maybe writ: flipped em-R-I-T."

"You know the name Flipped M is just a metaphor, right? The simplEng learning modality has flipped the classroom, giving students the ability to educate themselves and making learning English simpler by taking out the unnecessary complexities, such as the word *double-you*, which is the only letter in the alphabet that has more than one syllable and as such can be tricky for non-native speakers."

"That's interesting," I say. "So then is metaphor spelled: upside down double you-E-T-A-P-H-O-R?"

"I'm sensing some cynicism," he says with a smile.

"It's not cynicism…more like pragmatism, as someone I once knew used to say."

"Do you still listen to that message of his every night?"

"Do you still ask questions you already know the answers to?" I ask.

"I wonder what he'd be like if he were alive today…I'm sure he'd be the best of us."

"I imagine he'd think you were the best of us," I say. "After all, you're the one who's changed the most."

"But it took me so long just to get to where everyone else starts."

"When measuring your life's journey, it's the distance traveled that counts—not the time it took to get there."

"That sounds very Zen…or Hallmark," he says. "I'm not sure which, but I am sure that I couldn't have made it this far without your help."

"I've done less than I should have," I tell him. "I'm the one who deserves to be here."

"I deserve to be here not for the things I did but for the things I wanted to do but lacked the resolve."

"No one deserves to lose twenty years of their life for nothing," I say.

"I've gained much more than I've lost due to the time I've gotten to spend with you. What you did was far from nothing. You saved a man's life by taking it. With all the terrible things I imagined doing, I never once thought of that. You showed me grace."

He caresses my cheek with the back of his fingers. This sort of touching is not permitted, but the nearby guard appears not to notice.

Chapter Six

I no longer have the fear of a child, but as an adult I rarely do anything that frightens me. I no longer have childlike fantasies about how my life might one day be, and so I am better able to appreciate the moment, though each is tinged with the knowledge that fewer moments lay before me than behind.

In this newspaper's crossword puzzle, as in all newspapers, you will not find any clues referencing topics untoward or unseemly. The editors feel that such an inclusion would put you off your morning coffee or make your commute by rail all the more unpleasant. I don't want to add unpleasantness to your day either. After all, you have the Politics and Current Events sections for that, with the Business and Sports sections often rounding out the day's unpleasant news.

As a new columnist for this paper, I'd like to offer you a few bright paragraphs that perhaps cause the corners of your mouth to turn upwards and in the process make you want to read my future columns in these pages. So then why would I spoil any hope of a congenial introduction by telling you that nothing frightens me anymore because I am aware that this is as good as it gets, and I might as well enjoy it before I die?

Be sure to read my next column for the answer.

Just joking dear reader. I wouldn't do that to you, but frankly I don't think it matters what I write here. For instance: Presto CLASJO—Ilantro, Ime, Vocado, Alt, Alalpeno, Nion. See, you're still reading and that didn't make any sense at all. (Actually, it's an incantation for guacamole, but you'll need a cauldron and a big spoon, or at least a molcajete and pestle, to make it come out right.)

The truth is you're reading this newspaper because you're an addict for good news, which is really the only kind of news any paper has to offer. There's the good news that happens to us all and the bad news that happens to others, which is good news because it didn't happen to you or me.

As with all addicts, we are thankful for the daily dose of our drug of choice: the newest news. But I ask you, does the incessantly breaking news distract us from what has managed to remain unbroken? Does the alcoholic still savor the taste of good wine? Can the chain smoker still appreciate the smell of fresh air?

I hope to find an answer to these questions in the columns to come with, what I've been told is, my unique perspective. Perhaps I do see the world a little differently than you, and my point of view can offer a respite from the endless news that while ever changing always feels a little bit the same. Though maybe my outlook isn't so different from yours, in which case I think you'll find it enjoyable to read from a kindred soul now and then.

Either way, you have my promise that I won't report the news in this column. I wouldn't know how. Instead, I'll share with you that which isn't newsworthy, but that which I believe shouldn't be overlooked. And so I hope this will suffice as my congenial introduction.

Chapter Seven

Honking horns. Patty and I are driving to a big mall in some snub-burb...I don't know why. The city is confusing enough, but the suburbs are absolutely confounding. They go on and on—the next one always looking almost identical to the one you just left. I can only tell that we've entered a new suburb when the sequence of chain restaurants begins to repeat.

Patty had called an hour ago to ask if I wanted to go for a drive. I said sure, thinking she meant on some future day. Then she told me she was a few blocks away and would pick me up in five minutes. I didn't even know she had a car. It seems like a luxury model, so maybe it's Digy's, but then most cars seem luxurious compared to the cheap subcompacts that I usually rent.

She hasn't said much since she picked me up, keeping her attention on the slushy roads and the gray horizon. Maybe she's a nervous driver, but then why she wants to drive out to a suburban mall when she has VIP status at several clothing boutiques in her trendy neighborhood is beyond me.

Besides, she knows I hate shopping. I buy all my clothes online, and if I happen to find something that fits and feels comfortable, I order ten more of them. When I was first starting out, I mused about becoming a writer of such stature that I could get away with wearing the same outfit all the time like Mark Twain or Tom Wolfe, though I think if I wore their signature white suit I'd end up looking more like a Bee Gee. Now instead I just look like a crackpot who's too cheap to buy new clothes, which isn't exactly inaccurate since I tend to be parsimonious due to my frequent impecuniosity, and regrettably big words don't take the sting out of being poor.

To get the conversation going again after the few curt pleasantries she offered when I got in the car, I ask how she liked my first column.

"I thought it was good," she answers vaguely as she signals to pass a slow-moving minivan.

"Which part did you like best?" I press.

"Uh…the middle."

"Oh, that bit about the tiger."

"Yes, that was very surprising," Patty says.

I consider the slight pang of disappointment caused by my closest friend not having read my first column as an indicator of emotional growth. I decide to cut her some slack though, as I'm sure she must be very busy with the supervising of the nannies and the not working. She pulls into a parking lot the size of an airport. In the distance is the mall that looks like a ranch house for giants. The enormous lot is mostly empty. I imagine the only people willing to suffer the January roads to come to this mall, aside from its workers, are those with holiday returns, new gift cards, or cabin fever. She pulls into a spot far from the entrance or any other cars.

"Is this good?" she asks as she pushes the shifter into park.

"Sure, as long as you have two pairs of cross-country skis in the trunk."

"It makes me nervous to park next to other cars," she says as she opens her door. "Come on, the walk will be a good workout for us."

"Yeah, it'll really be a workout for you after I freeze to death and you have to slide me inside."

"What'd you say?" she asks, coming around from the other side of the car.

"I said give me a sec to put my mittens on."

We walk along the endless row of empty parking spaces, our feet crunching the rock salt and calcium chloride used to keep the lot from icing over. High above the frontage road stands a billboard depicting an image of three nubile, teenage girls prancing giddily with shopping bags from the mall we're trekking toward. The one in the middle wears a cute stocking cap and a tight sweater that doesn't quite cover her toned midriff, as if the stares of oglers will be enough to keep her warm.

"Why do they pander to the young?" Patty asks, her breath looking like cigarette smoke in the frigid air. "They don't have any money."

"Advertising skews young because it's more effective with them; older people just don't care as much," I answer. "Anyhow, pushy middle-aged women in parkas wouldn't be as eye catching."

"It'd be more honest."

"Right," I say, "because that's what advertising is all about."

"I was in public relations for almost two decades, so I know how advertising works, but if honesty is too much to ask for, then what about fairness?"

"Like the fairness of different eras prizing different types of beauty?" I ask. "In the Middle Ages those girls would've been mistaken for carriers of the plague. I suppose it evens out over history, but then it doesn't do anything for fat ladies today."

"No, I guess it doesn't."

"What do you have to worry about anyway?" I ask. "You're the prettiest person I know, and you haven't put on an ounce since college."

"I'm not sure about that."

"Sure you are," I accuse. "Listen, you seem like you want to talk, but you've barely said a word since you picked me up and dragged me out here."

"I'm sorry—"

"Don't be sorry, just tell me what's bothering you."

"I don't feel like myself anymore," Patty says. "I finally thought I had my transitioning under control, but lately I don't know who I am or what I want."

"You're not suffering from personality transitions; you're suffering from a midlife crisis. I know how you feel."

"Do you?" she asks. "I mean you've got your new job, your new place...a new start. I've got a lovely prison cell that I have to stay in if I want to be close to my son. Sure I can leave whenever I want. I can take a drive in a car that's probably bugged or go for a walk and probably be followed by somebody employed by my son's father."

"Oh, so that's why we're walking around out here in the middle of nowhere," I say, momentarily losing focus on my friend's emotions as I piece together the reasons for her actions. "The first thing we'll do is figure out how you would change your life if you could, and the next thing we'll do is figure out how you can."

I wait for her to say something as her eyes go all glassy, but instead she lunges at me, embracing me in a hard hug that I feel powerless to break free from without causing a spectacle. She knows I hate these demonstrative displays, and yet she continues on like an obstinate boa constrictor.

"Is this a lesbian thing?" I ask. "I know I just said you're attractive, but I'm barely a heterosexual. I'm nowhere near sophisticated enough to pull off being a homosexual."

"Don't make me laugh while I'm crying," she says as she lets me go and wipes her face with her gloved hand.

A pickup truck with big tires splashes past and slows to a stop just ahead of us. The mulleted driver rolls down his window, whistles, and then shouts, "You lesbos need a ride?"

"Kiss my whole ass, asshole!" I shout back as he spits and speeds off, parking in a handicap spot near the entrance that's still some distance away, though we've managed to make it to the more densely populated area of the parking lot.

"That's a funny thing to say," Patty tells me as we resume walking.

"Thanks, but I don't think it's the type of thing that'll catch on."

"I don't know," she says, "you're pretty plugged in."

"I'm not sure what you mean by that, but I'm flattered that you feel you can confide in me, though don't you have like a thousand other friends who are better at talking about these emotional issues?"

"I maybe know a thousand people, but sometimes I'm not sure if any of them but you are really my friend."

"That's strange that you know so many more people than me," I say, "and yet we have the same number of friends."

"It might seem strange to you, but for the rest of us I think it's pretty normal."

"So then you're saying I'm abnormal?"

"Yes, you're abnormal and wonderful," Patty answers. "You're not like any of us, but you understand so many things better than the rest of us, which is why people read your writing and why I value your counsel."

She's stops behind the tailgate of a large SUV. I'm afraid she's going to hug me again, but instead she only looks at me through watery eyes and smiles. I guess we're having another moment—any more of these and I'll need a drink. Suddenly the horn of the SUV honks. A middle-aged woman in a parka angrily approaches, beeping her key fob, aiming it at us like a pistol.

"You two get away from there."

"Shove it lady," Patty says.

"I'm in a hurry," the lady shouts as she pushes past us, "so you two can kiss my whole ass, assholes!"

"Where on Earth did you hear that?" Patty asks sardonically.

"From some dumb redneck getting out of a giant truck," she answers as she climbs into her own oversized vehicle. "This used to be a nice mall for decent people…now move along before I back over you."

We laugh harder than we have in a long time and then do as we're told.

Chapter Eight

Bump in the night. "Really?" I think to myself as I open my eyes. Light from a passing elevated train at the end of the alley flickers through the diaphanous curtains of my dark bedroom. I just got to sleep what feels like ten minutes ago after tossing and turning for over an hour, trying to think of what to write for my next column. The alarm clock's angry red numbers tell me that I've been asleep for nearly three hours.

Did I really hear a noise or was it just something from an unremembered dream that woke me up? I strain to listen. Then I hear it again, like the sound of an intruder entering a house—first a quiet noise followed quickly by a loud one. It's a low hissing and then a hard thud, as if a metal fist knocked once on a door down the hallway. The sound echoes through the corridor, like the explosive report of a gun fired in a narrow canyon.

I sit up in bed and consider my options. My bat is by the door, and I'm not sure where I left my phone. My door is locked. My floors are creaky when it's cold outside. Again, I can't help but think that a new construction shouldn't have creaky floors. Focus. If I get my bat or go look for my phone, whoever is out there may hear me walking across the living room. If I don't get my bat or my phone, and the prowler breaks down my door, then it'll just be me in my flannel pajamas defending myself against who knows who with no help on the way. There are twelve units on this level. As loud as that banging noise in the middle of the night seems, it doesn't sound as loud as a door being kicked in, so I'll stay quiet and wait to hear if whoever's out there starts kicking in doors. If he does begin entering units, there's less than a one in ten chance that he'll start with mine, so I should have an opportunity to find my phone, call the police, put on some pants, and grab my burglar beater.

The hissing noise and hard knock draw closer to my unit. It continues a few more times until finally I hear the prowler just outside my door—a low hiss followed by a loud bang. Then he continues on down the hallway. I've counted the combination of hiss and bang sounds nine times now, so maybe he only has three more doors to do...whatever it is that he's doing. Or maybe I missed the first couple before I woke. Or maybe I'm too keyed up to make an accurate tally. Either way, all is quiet again.

The alarm clock informs me several minutes have passed, though of course it feels like much longer. I listen hard for the sound of the heavy glass door downstairs or for footsteps upstairs, but I don't hear anything at all. I don't think I could hear something that far away from inside my bedroom, and it's possible the prowler moved on during the noise of the last train that passed a few minutes ago, or it's possible he's waiting for someone to come out into the hallway.

Now is one of those moments when I miss my old roommate most—not because I thought he could protect me, but because we could be scared together. I hug my pillow and somehow manage to fall back asleep.

It's after ten o'clock when I wake up again. The midmorning sun fills my bedroom with light. Even though I hardly ever have anything pressing to get out of bed for, I can't remember the last time I slept in so late…probably not since my twenties. It takes me a minute to remember why I must've been so tired, then it all comes back to me at once.

I noiselessly pull on my most comfortable pair of jeans and an old sweatshirt. Aside from a garbage truck in the alley, all is quiet in the building. I tiptoe barefoot to my door and look out the peek-hole…that doesn't sound right. I've keyed myself up into a half-stupid state again. Something is partially obstructing my view into the hallway. I can only see down to the floor, but the thin hallway carpet looks the same, though what was I expecting to see on the floor…bloody footprints perhaps? I drop to the floor and look under my door to confirm…there's no blood. I have no idea what I'm doing. I should've brewed some coffee first, though that might've made me all the more jittery.

I grab my bat, open my door, and steel myself for one of the thirty possibilities that my imagination has worked up since last night. What I find doesn't match any of them. A red rose has been affixed to my door with a four-penny nail just above the peephole—that's the right word—and a heart shape has been sloppily spray painted around it. I look up and down the hallway; each door has received the same treatment—a dozen red roses circumscribed by loopy black hearts.

Great, I have a secret admirer/terrorizer, who's probably crazy and certainly an awful artist. At least this will give credence to the condo management's hypothesis that vandals are somehow getting into the building.

I hear my phone ringing. Where did I leave it? I go back inside and listen for the next ring. I should leave it on my nightstand next to my flashlight when I go to bed, but that rarely happens. Usually I fall asleep on the couch in front of the television, so it ends up behind a cushion, and I forget all about it when I finally drag myself to bed. Another ring…it's not coming from the living room. Now I remember—I left it in the kitchen when I was eating stale cookies over the sink as a late-night snack…quite a charmed life I live.

I pick the phone up from the counter just as the ringing stops and the screen indicates the caller has been sent to voice-mail. I rinse cookie crumbs down the drain as I wait for the message icon to appear. I tap the icon on my screen when it finally pops up, and I hear my editor's voice.

"Vivien, your first column has been generated a fair amount of buzz over the last couple of days—nicely done. Now when will you be sending me the next one?"

It's been a long time since I've gotten a phone message from someone inquiring about the progress of a writing assignment. I feel both a calm sense of wistfulness and a harried sense of exigency, but mostly I feel hungry. How can I be expected to write on an empty stomach? After all, a girl's gotta eat. I'm sure this is one of those instances when my old thesis advisor would've called me dear.

Chapter Nine

In line? On line? I've lived all over the country, so I can't re-member which it is that they say here. Am I waiting in a line at the deli to order a sandwich, or on a line? On line makes me think of the Internet but then in line makes me think of rollerblades…I miss those. I must be hungry; my thoughts are all over the place. I should be thinking of what I'm going to write for my next column, or who might've broken into my building, or at least what I'm going to order. So far I've nar-rowed it down to one of everything.

The two charming gentlemen in front of me, with all the manners of bank robbers, are having an enlightened conver-sation that, try as I might, I can't ignore. If men are so intent on objectifying women, couldn't they at least do so in a less obvious way? These philistines might as well be talking about the weather. Big boobs and sunshine good, thick waists and rainstorms bad.

"So you ask the masseuse before you turn over and take off your towel?"

"I always ask…I just don't care what the answer is. I told this one that I'd show her four inches but that she'd have to earn the fifth and sixth."

"What'd she say?"

"She said she'd settle for two inches and a backrub in return."

"So did she give you a hand?"

"Why do you think I tipped forty percent? I'm telling you, the place is a sure thing and the girls are knockouts. All you have to do is tell them you've been there before."

"Won't they know that I haven't?"

"It doesn't matter…they don't care…it's just like their secret code."

"Did you really give her a massage afterwards?"

"No, that was just a joke."

"Well, it sounds like a swanky joint, but I think I'll stick with my regular place. I always feel comfortable there."

"They'll make you feel comfortable here too. You should branch out and try something new."

"Nah, I like my place."

"That's exactly what I'm saying—you can like your place and this new spot. Let's pretend for a minute that you have two testicles. You wouldn't like one and not the other…you'd like them both. Maybe you'd like the one that hangs lower a little less, but it wouldn't be as if to prefer one you had to hate the other."

"That's true…I mean it's not true what you implied about me not having any balls, but I see your point about liking two different places. Anyway, I'm starving. What are you going to order?"

"I haven't been this hungry since the Holocaust, so I'm going to order a double-decker submarine."

The old woman in front of them turns and glowers. One of them shrugs and the other tells her to mind her own business. They resume their classy conversation. That's the thing with jackasses—they're proud to be a jackass, and they feed off others seeing them as such, which only perpetuates the appalling cycle of jackassery.

As they leave I tell them that I hope they both enjoy stuffing their penis-shaped sandwiches into their mouths. One calls me a bitch and the other something worse. What did I expect? At least now I have something to write about for my column.

Chapter Ten

I'd like you to participate in a thought experiment with me to help assay a theory I came up with after a recent contretemps. Imagine the last rude stranger that you encountered. Maybe the rowdy guy on the train or the pushy woman in the store, but some jackass that made you angry as hell and that you never saw again. (I know, so much for my second column being upbeat and bouncy.)

Before we go any further, let me calibrate our understanding of humans by asking if you agree with these two statements: it's easier for people to accept the unfairness of circumstances than the unfairness of aptitude, and it's not difficult to convince people of their exceptionalism.

I figured our thinking on those two points would be congruent. If you're like me, typically when you do something wrong you do it out of raw emotion (cursing in front of children at a chancy cyclist on a sidewalk) or a misguided sense of what's right (puncturing said cyclist's tires when you find his bike chained up a block away in hopes of teaching him a lesson). On my best days I don't intentionally do something I know is wrong, and when I do commit a solecism I don't try to rationalize it, but instead I try to learn from it. At the rate I'm going, I'll have learned everything I need to know about ten minutes before I die.

But I digress, so now back to the jackasses. There are those who will tell you that these asses deserve the benefit of the doubt, and certainly some of them probably do. But not all of them…maybe not most of them. When an ass in an automobile passes me on the shoulder of the expressway and then cuts me off, I used to imagine that the ass was on his way to the hospital for an emergency or that the ass was in urgent need of a restroom, but then sometimes I would see that same ass farther down the road, cheerily chatting on a cellphone. My infuriation would redouble since not only did the ass perpetrate his transgression but then I lied to myself by concocting a scenario to justify his offense. I submit that this whole business of giving jackasses the benefit of the doubt is at best a wash and at worst self-delusion.

I do believe though that self-delusion is at the root of the issue, and in this regard jackasses are our betters…at least partly. After all, a jackass knows he's a jackass, and he's fine with it, which is part of his jackassedness. However, in another, more important way, the jackass is sorely lacking in personal perspicacity. See the asses have convinced themselves that their boorish behavior is acceptable, even warranted perhaps, either because they believe they have been treated unfairly in life by the cards they've been dealt and so are owed a reprieve from the rules or because they have been dealt such good cards that they feel as if they ought to win every hand and so are above the rules. Whatever the reason, the result is the same: jackasses simply don't value the social mores that the rest of us comply with so that we might live in a functional society.

To those who refuse to respect our culture's standards, I say keep jackassing…for the following two reasons: a social cancer is the only cancer that can cure itself, and the best test of good manners is to be patient when confronted with bad manners. As the hordes of jackasses seem to grow inexorably and even exponentially, we, the well-mannered (or in my case, one who tries to be), will have ever increasing opportunities to hone our skills at suffering the asses. I think eventually, if we are diligent in our training, we'll begin to perceive their inevitable misconduct like inclement weather—not something to be avoided altogether but rather something to be coped with and tolerated.

And as their obdurate ranks continue to increase geometrically, in part due to the presumed softness of those of us who repudiate the policy of fighting fire with fire and so refuse to play their dishonorable game to keep them in check, they will more and more find themselves at odds with the multiplying legions of other asses, for a jackass is most pleased with himself when he's inveighing against a person he regards as a contemptible cipher, such as a fellow jackass. Long ago I witnessed a confrontation between two obstreperous moviegoers after the first's noisy perseverations at the screen prompted the second to shout at him, "You think being loud is the same as being interesting. Do you know who always thinks the loudest person is the most interesting? The guy who's the loudest and nobody else, so shut up! No one here bought a ticket to listen to an annoying loudmouth." Indeed.

When we have mastered attenuating the impact of a jackass's rudeness by responding with forbearance, we'll have deprived the offender of what he most wants, compelling him to seek out his own kind for the conflict he craves. And in the eyes of those dissolute churls he will see his own reflection; in the sounds of the epithets and profanities hurled at him he will hear echoes of the words he has spoken before. Ultimately he will be forced to ask himself how the world went so wrong.

You and I will understand. We'll offer the knowing smile of a veteran to a rookie, and if my theory proves correct, then one day he too might learn to live with decency above the degradation, but it'll take patience and practice and that arduous education will be his comeuppance, which for us will probably feel something like the satisfaction a plumber gets when he quotes a lawyer his hourly rate. I believe the key to solving the jackass epidemic that currently besieges our civilization, and I'm paraphrasing something an old friend used to say, is to let the problem of the asses become the solution of the asses.

Chapter Eleven

Glover. If you'd asked me a week ago, I would've guessed that Glover was the name of a Muppet, but Patty informed me it's what you call someone who is skilled at making gloves—I suppose that makes more sense than a cobbler. Last time I went shopping with Patty she took exception to my mittens and insisted that she would have a pair made for me by her favorite glover. When I protested, she called my mittens frowzy, but then I explained that my mittens had kept my fingers from getting frowzy for many years.

The glover's assistant—I imagine when making gloves one usually needs a hand...like your jokes are so great—greeted Patty warmly and told us that the glover was out but that he'd return shortly. He suggested we have a look at the store's samples to find some styles to our liking, and so here we are perusing the wares of Glover's Lane.

"What about these?" Patty asks, holding up a handsome, calfskin pair that look as snug-fitting as evening gloves.

"I need more room for my hands to breathe," I answer, "the way my mittens do."

"Why do you like those tattered old mittens so much?"

"My hands have normal hydration in the winter, and by that I mean the skin on the back of my hands gets so dry that my knuckles crack and bleed, but if I wear gloves my palms get so sweaty that I'm embarrassed when I take them off and have to shake hands, so it evens out to normal. In addition to keeping my hands warm, the faux fur lining of my mittens absorbs and redistributes the excess moisture from my palms to the back of my hands."

"Wow," Patty says.

"I know, they work pretty well."

"No," she clarifies. "I mean wow that's disgusting."

"We can't all have flawless, porcelain skin."

"I have good skin because I take care of myself."

"So do I."

"What brand of moisturizer do you use?" Patty asks.

"I...I..."

"Come on, lotion...night cream...anything."

"I eat right."

"Name a vegetable in your refrigerator right now."

"That's a trick question," I say, "you don't put vegetables in the refrigerator."

"You put them in the crisper drawer because they require higher humidity levels to stay fresh," Patty explains imperiously. "What do you keep in your crisper drawer?"

"Uh, usually European leftovers that I don't want getting mushy...you know, like French fries and Belgian waffles. If that's not what a crisper drawer is for, then where should I put that stuff?"

"In the garbage."

"Listen, I'm in good health." I have a pair of driving gloves clenched in my hand that I'm considering using to slap Patty across the face with so as to initiate a duel.

"Who says so?" Patty asks.

"My doctor."

"When was the last time you went for a checkup?"

"For your information, I have an appointment with a gynecologist later this week."

"I didn't ask when your next checkup will be," she says. "I asked when your last checkup was."

"It's been a few years, okay?" I brush the hair away from my forehead as I feel my face grow warm. "Now that I'm working again I've got my health insurance back. Who are you trying to be, anyway...my mother?"

"Maybe." Her face suddenly gets as flush as mine feels, but then her color returns to normal as she slowly exhales. I'm not sure if she had a personality transition or if she just calmed herself down because she saw that I was getting worked up. Perhaps she's micro-transitioning these days. Is that a thing?

"My mentioning the word 'mother' seemed to hit a nerve," I say.

"I guess it did," Patty replies. "I've been feeling a bit like a zombie mommy of late. With all my son's nannies, each of whom has a graduate degree in early childhood education, I'm not sure what my role is anymore."

"They're not keeping you from him, are they?"

"No, of course not," Patty answers. "I would never allow that...but they're always around. Don't get me wrong...they're great with my boy, and he loves them all, so I don't want to dismiss them, but I feel like they're assessing me as much as him, reporting everything back to Digy."

"That sounds a little paranoid," I say, "but not completely implausible."

"Oh, I don't care what they tell him...not really. I just don't know what I'm supposed to be doing. I feel like I'm wandering from room to room, seeing if I'm needed anywhere, haunting my son like the undead."

"If I'm not mistaken, zombies are dead, vampires are undead, and ghosts haunt," I offer, trying to introduce a little levity. "So that's why you've been wanting to shop so much lately—why you've been smothering…I mean mothering me."

"I suppose it's my smotherly instincts spilling over," Patty says with a laugh. "By the way, I believe anything that has ceased living but continues to move about under its own power is considered undead."

"That's not what's troubling you is it…fear of growing old and dying?" I ask. "For me the trick to aging well is to stay interesting…bores age more quickly. Young people are interesting, at least they think they are, because they have the potential to be anything; however, by the time they get to be our age their potential has narrowed…but that's not so with us. I move and get a new job every couple of years, and you have it made. With your experience and financial freedom, you could do whatever you want."

"You're being asinine," Patty replies. "The trick to aging well isn't a trick at all, but what we were just talking about: taking care of your skin, eating healthy, and getting regular medical checkups. It's like you haven't been paying attention. And anyway, I don't have a fear of death…maybe a fear of not living…perhaps a fear of not having a purpose."

"You're a mother…what larger purpose is there?" I ask.

"Again, I feel like you're not hearing me. I'm a mother surrounded by women who are better at raising a child than I could ever hope to be."

"But they're not your son's mother. Also, I heard you fine the first time, and I think you're being an ass to the nines. So you've got some help raising your child. I'm sure most mothers wish they had more—take the win. Part of a parent's role is to care for her child; the other part is to give her child a connection to the person who came before him and an inkling of the person he can expect to grow into so that he can model himself after you and maybe even learn from your mistakes—nobody can do that better for a child than a parent."

She stares at me with a lopsided grin that looks as if it's objective is to keep the chin below it from quivering. Her eyes have gone all watery again. Must we do this every time we get together? She hugs me hard. I pat her on the back and resist the temptation to sarcastically say: there, there.

"Thank you," Patty says as she begins to sob. She cries on my shoulder. I wish I had my mittens handy so that I could turn them inside out and use them to absorb her tears; however, as much as I detest these emotional displays, I must admit that it's nice to have a friend.

"This all feels very familiar," I say, trying to lighten the mood and put an end to the waterworks.

"Yes," Patty agrees as she lets go of me. "All we need now is for a woman in a parka to tell us that we're each being an ass to the nines."

Chapter Twelve

Naming trees. It's something I do. I can't stand when people introduce themselves with more than one name: Hi, my name is Margaret, but you can call me Maggie, Margie, Megan, Peggy, Gretchen, or Rita. Just tell me your name is Rita; it's not like I'll be checking your ID later. But I've wandered…I tend to do that when I talk to myself. I think we ought to take all the extra, superfluous names of Homo tautologous and give them to trees. I wonder if we named trees, would we take better care of them? Or maybe first we'd have to care about them more for us to then feel obliged to name them. Although there are plenty of people with names who I couldn't care less about, so maybe one doesn't have anything to do with the other.

I like trees most when they're bare. It's easy to appreciate trees in summer when they're teeming with leaves, but I think trees are at their best in the wintertime when they're unadorned skeletons. It's remarkable that trees divest themselves of their foliaged clothing when they need it the most and somehow survive the cold months in their nakedness, as if taunting the winter to do its worst to their exposed bones, only to survive and flourish again come springtime. I'm sitting under an Acer palmatum, a Japanese maple, in a park I've grown quite fond of, trying to think of a good name for this tree, but the ground is algid, and my bottom is freezing, so I'm having difficulty focusing.

The water close to the bank of the nearby lake had been frozen solid, but then thawed and cracked, causing sheets of ice to collide into one another, and has since refrozen so that in spots the ice sheets have formed triangular temples. I like parks in winter when no one else is around, and it's as quiet as a church on Monday. I think the trees appreciate my presence, standing at attention and waiting for me to review them, like soldiers engaged in a long battle deriving comfort from a commanding officer taking the time to inspect their ranks. My communion with the trees is such that I feel—

My mobile phone rings, snapping me out of my reverie. I pull it from my coat pocket. It's my editor calling. I suppose I ought to answer it. After all, I came here to think of something to write about for my next column. I tap the touchscreen with the phone-friendly, silk fingertip of my new gloves. Perhaps she'll have some words of encouragement to offer.

"Hello."

"You lied to me," she says crossly. So much for encouragement.

"Okay…about what, exactly?"

"The Prodigy character in that little book of yours…Digy you called him. He and the founder of the Flipped M School I asked you about are one and the same."

"I didn't use real names in my book to…I don't know… protect the truth," I say defensively. "That's not against the law."

"Neither is firing you for lying during an interview."

"I never said for sure it wasn't him."

"Don't play games with me," she scolds. "You told me you hadn't seen your classmates in years, but I have it on good authority you just saw him recently."

"Yes, right after my interview. Before that I hadn't seen him since college."

"But you are friends with the mother of his child," she says. "I presume the Patty person you described in your book."

"How do you know all this?" I ask.

"Your Digy is one of the most influential people in the world, and he happens to live right in our backyard, but he never grants interviews, so I have reporters keep a pretty close eye on him."

"What does that have to do with me? I mean I know him, but we're not friends or anything."

"Yes, but you are friends with someone very close to him."

"Listen," I say, "There's no way I'm going to leverage my relationship with Patty just to get you an interview with—"

"Hold on," she interrupts, taking the sharpness out of her voice. "I wasn't going to ask you to use your friend to get an interview with her baby's father, even if it would be the biggest exclusive interview this flagging newspaper ever had—a boon to us all."

"Then what were you going to ask me?"

"The Flipped M School is holding a presser today. I doubt your so-called Prodigy will be there; he hardly ever attends press conferences. Nevertheless, I want you to go down there and write about it for your next column."

"Don't you have other people for this sort of thing?" I ask with a voice more whiny than I want it to be. "I'm not a reporter, you know."

"I'll be sending my usual reporters that cover these types of events, and I'm sure they'll write the usual things, but with your background you could offer a unique perspective in your column."

"I don't know."

"Then let me ask you something else," she says. "What were you planning to write for your next column? It's been a few days since your last one."

"I was just finalizing it now," I say faintly.

"What's it about?"

"Well, it's still a little rough."

"What's it about…roughly?" she asks.

"Okay, I'll go to the presser, but I'm not writing about Patty or anything to do with her personal life."

"Fine," she says, "have it in my inbox by the end of the day."

She hangs up before I can tap the button on my screen to end the call—one advantage of an old-fashioned phone. I stand up and brush the dead-leaf detritus from my backside. The crumbled, burgundy pieces look much darker than the bright red leaves that must've once adorned this tree. I name this maple Akai for its Asian roots.

Chapter Thirteen

Bleeding edge, not blending in. Clearly that's what the Flipped M School is aiming for, judging by its not-so-subtle mission statement inscribed in the large plaque on the wall behind the reception desk at the main entrance:

If you don't know us, you will. Soon our name will be illuminated on the screens of every mobile device read by passengers of public transportation. You say you don't take public transportation. Do you fly? You say not commercial. Then yes, you may miss the revolution…or at least its uprise.

-Your Friends at the Flipped M School

From what I understand, this neo-Gothic tower was once the headquarters for the rival of the newspaper I write for, until it was forced to downsize and move its offices to a building named for an insurance company located in the less fashionable part of the downtown area. Now Digy's for-profit college is headquartered here. I knew that kid when he used to get pimples on his face the size of ladybugs.

"Hello," I say to the young man sitting behind the desk. "I'm here for this afternoon's presser."

"Congratulations," he says indifferently without looking up from the monitor in front of him.

"Listen you snarky slacker, why don't you try doing your job and tell me where it's being held."

"You must be new," he says with a smirk. "Go past the elevators and take a left. It's in the conference hall."

"Thanks, you've been somewhat helpful."

I make my way to the conference hall and slip in with the last few late arrivals. It's standing room only in the back of the hall. Up front on the dais, behind the lectern, stands a bespectacled, balding man with a neatly groomed beard, wearing a houndstooth blazer over a black turtleneck. He clears his throat into the microphone, the hall quiets down, and he begins to speak.

"Thank you for coming this afternoon. I see some familiar faces here in the front and some new faces there in the back—welcome one and all. Without further ado, let me get right to the point, but first I'll take a moment to give you some context for today's exciting announcement.

"As I'm sure you all know, the founder of our MOOC—that is Massive Open Online College—is also the creator of simplEng, which was his first foray into education on a global scale. As Third-World literacy rates continue to climb and our planet moves ever closer to speaking in a single tongue, I think we can all agree that simplEng has been an enormous success...and I think you'll also come to agree that the Flipped M School's next venture will be capable of equaling, if not exceeding, the enormity of that success."

Without consciously willing it, I feel my arm shoot up to ask a question. I can tell I've caught the speaker's attention as he looks down at his tablet computer but hesitates before pressing on and then looks up again. "I see a hand in the back. Usually we save our questions until the end, but I see that the hand belongs to one of the new faces I mentioned at the outset, so with a welcoming attitude I will answer your question now."

"Thanks," I say. "Did you mean 'enormousness' when you said 'enormity' a moment ago? Because I think they mean different things."

A few people toward the front snicker. A woman next to me using her phone to record what's being said shakes her head. "Ah, you are very new indeed," says the speaker patronizingly. He must've been hired by Digy personally.

"This is a perfect opportunity for a teachable moment," continues the snooty speaker, lecturing directly at me. "Thanks to simplEng the word 'enormousness' no longer exists."

"But of course it still exists," I say, cutting into his disquisition, "I just said it and then you repeated it."

"Be that as it may," the speaker begins again, "'Enorm—' that word has been eradicated from the simplEng vocabulary in favor of 'enormity,' which is shorter."

"But they don't mean the same thing," I protest. "'Enormousness means big, and 'enormity' means evil."

"Yes, well they both mean the same thing in simplEng."

"Didn't you just tell me that 'enormousness' doesn't exist in simplEng?"

"We're talking in circles now, and I want to be respectful of everyone's time, so let's table this discussion and move on, but suffice it to say that your comments typify precisely the lack of clarity that simplEng was created to correct. After all, why have a language with so many similar words that have different meanings and so many different words that have similar meanings when you can just have simplEng? And so I thank you for the question, as it provides a perfect segue back to what I was saying before.

"As I'm sure you recall, simplEng was developed after many years of exhausting research—"

My hand shoots up again, and I say without waiting to be called on, "I think you mean 'exhaustive.'"

"It's the same as before," says the speaker. "'Exhausting' replaced 'exhaustive'…it's simpler."

"How's it simpler?" I ask. "They have the same number of letters."

"Let's not get cute," he says as he attempts to stifle his ire. "Continuing on, after exhaust…uh, extensive research it was established that it takes about forty hours to read a collegiate dictionary from cover to cover. The simplEng dictionary can be read in ten. And so in that same spirit of culling needless information in order to reduce the duration of an educational experience by three quarters, we are pleased to announce our new one-year bachelor's degree program."

With this every hand in the room but mine shoots up simultaneously.

"Yes, yes," the speaker resumes as the murmuring abates, "many questions I'm sure. Permit me to answer some of the more obvious ones now, lest we go too far too soon into the weeds on some of the finer points.

"Firstly, this bachelor's program will be free to all, just as all the Flipped M School's programs of study are. Secondly, this bachelor's program is but the initial offering of our new initiative; expect many more programs to become available in the weeks to come, including a six-month master's degree, and a nine-month PhD program—we believe if you can grow a baby in nine months, then you ought to be able to earn a doctorate in the same amount of time. Thirdly, our programs have been preapproved for accreditation by several multinational institutions that the Flipped M School has enjoyed longstanding relationships with, and we look forward to growing those synergistic associations."

Once more many hands shoot up. The speaker scans the group, looking for someone to call on. "You there from the Journal…go ahead."

"You say that this new, shorter bachelor's program will be free like all your other programs. Do you then plan to monetize it in the same way as the others?"

"I'm tempted to blithely respond, 'if it ain't broke don't fix it,'" the speaker says with a toothy smile. "Yes, we'll continue to offer advertisements for quality products from reputable brands alongside our educational content, which in turn will generate vast sums of tax revenue, unlike those nonprofit universities that receive endless endowments and yet never pay a dime in taxes. Remember, for many of our long-distance learners in Third-World countries, these ads are their first exposure to First-World merchandise, so although these truncated programs will offer less time for advertising overall, we believe that this evanescence will present an appealing opportunity for advertisers—consider the premium costs paid for Super Bowl commercials."

Without raising my hand, I shout out a simple question. "Excuse me, did you say 'appalling opportunity'?"

The speaker glares at me as all the heads in the room turn in my direction. Somewhere, someone chuckles.

"No, I said 'appealing opportunity.'"

"My mistake," I say. "I must've misheard you."

"Very well, now back to other questions…uh, yes you from the Times."

"You mentioned future graduate programs that the Flipped M School will be rolling out. Often PhD candidates try to get their dissertations published. I'm sure eager students will sign up for your new graduate programs in droves, but will academic publications be capable of handling the attendant increase in submissions?"

"Excellent question—I assure you that's an issue we've thought about for some time…we really deliberated over it. Our solution is as elegant as it is practical. We've partnered with other online universities, so as to keep the competition lively, to create a repository of knowledge, if you will. This will be an elite, online library to which we anticipate some of the best academic papers will be submitted and assessed through our proprietary, crowdsourced, peer-review process; however, since inclusion is at the core of our mission, the library will also house every digital submission we receive in a searchable database. We predict that within months our virtual library will swell in size to become the largest collection of academic papers in all of human history, and as an added bonus, since all of the library's publications will only be available in an electronic format, nary a tree shall perish."

I blurt out, "What's the name of this suppository of knowledge?"

"Miss, that's 'repository of knowledge,'" the speaker says over a few more chuckles and one outright guffaw.

"My mistake again…this simplEng business has me so confused."

"To be clear," the speaker says slowly as his face changes color from pink to red, "simplEng sounds the same as old…I mean…traditional English. There are just fewer words, some changes to definitions, and less conjugating of verbs…simplEng doesn't concern itself with pronunciation."

"Got it—great…thanks," I say, "but what's the name of this repository?"

The speaker looks down and grumpily swipes the screen of his tablet. "It seems I…uh…don't have the name in front of me at the moment, but I'm certain whatever it is that it's inspiring."

"I'm sure of it," I say, trying not to betray too much sarcasm. "It was probably hard coming up with a name while being distracted by all that deliberating."

More laughter erupts. The woman near me using her phone to record the conference moves it in my direction.

"It's time to hear from someone else," the speaker says sternly. "You there from the Post."

"You said 'preapproved for accreditation' by 'multinational institutions.' Could you please elaborate?"

"I'd be happy to…based on our distinguished track record of offering top-tier educational opportunities to traditionally underserved communities, we've been granted accreditation in advance for our new programs so that we can start enrolling our students sooner."

"Sorry," I break in, "when did you say your students will start eye rolling?"

The speaker speaks on, either pretending that he didn't hear me or that I don't exist. "As for the multinational institutions, these are renowned organizations that are based in various countries across the globe, many of which our students live in."

"Many of your students also live here in the states," the reporter from the Post follows up. "Are any of these academic accrediting bodies located here?"

"I'm glad you asked that," says the speaker, looking as if he's trying to suppress the urge to squirm. "For years the Flipped M School has attempted to work with domestic, government-run accrediting agencies, but time and time again we've found their unwillingness to evaluate our courses and programs on their unique merits—preferring instead to use their standardized metrics that are antiquated and inflexible—to be a hindrance to the progress of both our school and our students. As such, when it comes to the process of seeking accreditation, we've chosen to readjust."

"Pardon me," I ask loudly, "do you mean that these foreign, puppet agencies 'read just' what you tell them to when they announce your accreditation?"

"'Readjust' and 'read just' don't even sound alike," says the speaker, wiping spittle from his face as he does his best to ignore the tittering coming from all corners of the room.

"The way it was explained to me," I say, "is that simplEng doesn't concern itself with pronunciation."

The room bursts into laughter. An old man near the front says, "She's got you there." The speaker appears on the verge of an apoplectic episode.

"Miss, who do you write for?" the speaker demands.

"My readers," I answer firmly. "Now, I've got just one last question for you."

"Shut up!" the speaker barks. "No more questions from you."

"Answer her question," someone shouts from the center of the room. "She answered yours."

"Fine," says the speaker, lowering his voice as he adjusts his glasses. "What's your final question then?"

"You began by telling us about the Flipped M School's first one-year bachelor's program that you'll soon be offering."

"Yes, I remember" says the seething speaker.

"But what is it?"

"How do you mean?"

"I mean what's it in...astronomy, zoology?" I ask. "Something in between?"

"Oh," says someone up front, "good question." The woman near me with the phone nods her head.

The speaker looks flummoxed. "Well..."

The same upfront person says, "So tell us what is it."

"Uh..." the speaker stammers sheepishly, "...Media Relations."

Chapter Fourteen

Pretend for a moment that money is god. Some worship and others don't, but that belief affects us all. We receive communion when we exchange money for the things we want. We evangelize when we give money to those in need…it's far-fetched but stay with me for a moment.

Now pretend, if you will, that instead of valuing money above all else, we value education. We hold ceremonies in which elders dressed in robes welcome younger members, after proving their worth, into their exalted ranks. We exchange proverbs extoling the virtues of learning, perhaps such as "give a man a fowl and he'll eat for a day, teach a man to fowl and he'll eat for a lifetime."

I know, both scenarios are pretty out there, and certainly each has its drawbacks; however, I think we can agree that neither is completely beyond the realm of possibility as far as an ideology for a viable, though hypothetical, society goes. Now I want you to imagine the utterly impossible: that we live in a polytheist society that worships both money and education, but we all have different views on which is greater. In this bizarre scenario we don't revere demigods but rather demagogues who have loads of money and are leaders of learning. In fact, some of the most powerful among them make their fortune through education.

I attended a press conference today for the new pet project of one such person—not a demagogue perhaps of Olympian magnitude, but certainly his organization wields considerable influence and he himself has a voice that echoes far and wide, though he usually speaks quietly and often says very little.

The presser itself was one of those we promise to be transparent as long as you promise to keep your eyes shut, or at least your mouths, types of affairs. You'll find better coverage of the event in other corners of this newspaper, but what I want to focus on here is the person pulling the strings.

You know this man. He reinvented our language, and everyone seems to be in agreement that it is much improved, though no one quite seems to agree on precisely what improvements have been made. As far as I can tell, these enhancements have to do with reducing the number of words in our language, by the outright deletion of some words and the conflating of definitions for others.

In this spirit of shrinking our language by combining words to create a more economical vocabulary, I humbly submit the following adjective for your consideration: *avarrant*, which is the combination of aberrant and avarice and is defined as abnormally greedy. I'm open to calling it *abarice*, if you prefer.

Another term I'd like to propose for our lexicon is the noun *aptirudeness* from rudeness and aptitude, for those whose superior ability is matched only by their boorishness. Allow me to use these two new words in a sentence so that you can determine if they pass muster: We tolerated his aptirudeness because of his avarrant intentions.

Hmm, maybe that doesn't work after all, since it doesn't seem rational that we we would put up with someone who believes himself to be our better and condescends to us accordingly, if his objective is to make money off of us—lots of money—by ruining our system of higher education when he could instead share his resources to help us repair it. This word-merging business is trickier than I thought. It's almost as if it doesn't make any sense at all.

Let's suspend our language-altering efforts for now and go back a few steps to think a bit more about our original, suppositional scenarios. It's been said (I assume) that we endow our gods with magnificent powers to explain why we aren't godlike. If we decided to choose, instead of invent, for our idols those whose achievements far exceed our own accomplishments, wouldn't we be inclined to envisage them with talents they might not actually possess in order to explain the disparity between our successes?

Wouldn't it stand to reason, if indeed reason can exist in such an improbable scenario, that the heavenly attainments of these idols has more to do with happenstance and serendipity than manifest destiny and innate wisdom? (I mean, the world's fastest sprinter isn't a thousand times faster runner than us, so then why would we assume that someone a thousand times richer than us is a thousand times smarter too?) Would, perhaps, such a culture be more disposed to misplaced hero worship if it were bored and hungry for new ideas, even if the new ideas were merely recycled concepts that had been heard before, albeit in different mediums. Wouldn't it behoove said culture to recognize that its demagogues have their own agendas that don't necessarily address the needs of the people? Shouldn't this conjectural culture accept that it's time to stop listening to such Svengalis?

Chapter Fifteen

Ringing that causes wringing. Specifically, the ringing of my mobile phone makes me want to wring my hands with anxiety. It's my editor. I half thought she wouldn't run my last column out of fear of ruffling the wrong feathers—I figured that's what she deserved for strong-arming me into an assignment I didn't feel comfortable with—but to my surprise, there it was in this morning's newspaper. As the business day draws to a close—the train I'm on is crowded with commuters returning home—her call doesn't come as a surprise to me. I suspect Digy has spent the day, once he was made aware of my lowly column, plotting to have my vulnerable paper absorbed and me spat out in the process. Wring: flipped em-R-I-N-G.

I take the call, and before she can speak I ask, "So what's the bad news?" Bad news never gets any better by sitting on it.

"No bad news here," she says. "Why, did you hear something?"

"Uh...no, I haven't heard anything."

"Even though it may sound like a threat to our job security since we're in the newspaper business, no news really is good news."

"So then why are you calling?" I ask.

"Right...why would we want to waste a bunch of time with small talk? Your column is getting a lot of feedback, most of it positive, so I want you to start writing a daily column for the paper."

"I don't know."

"You don't know what?" she asks. "This should be the part when you say 'thanks for the opportunity.'"

"Don't get me wrong, I enjoy writing my column, but doing it every day..."

"Is this you angling for a raise?"

"No," I answer, "it's not about the money."

"That's what someone looking for more money would say. I suppose since you've been working here for almost a fortnight and the paper is flush with funds, you're due for a raise—just let me get some numbers together first and then we'll talk."

"Did you know I knew Digy when you hired me?" For the first time I hear silence from her end of the line.

"I thought you might," she answers. "Why does it matter now?"

"Because I don't want to be your go-to-gal for writing dirt about Digy. It was a one-time thing."

"That works out well, since I got official word today that you're persona non grata for any future events held by the Flipped M School."

"Oh." I've never been banned from anything in my life; it feels strange...strangely good. "So you're not going to ask me to write about Digy anymore?"

"No, like you said, it was a one-time thing."

"Good."

"I'm glad you think so," she says. "I want you writing more columns for us because you seem to be plugged in— people identify with you."

"I have no idea how that's possible."

"Who can ever understand how these things work?" she asks, not waiting for an answer. "It's taken me my whole career just to be able to identify when it happens...figuring it out is beyond my ken."

"Okay, I've got some writing to do. We'll talk later about my raise, and boss...thanks for the opportunity."

She says "goodbye" but then stays on the line so that I can end the call. I've never gotten a raise before. An old woman sitting next to me smiles at my good fortune. I must've been talking louder than I realized. The man sitting across from me wearing baggy pants and a hoodie pulled down low seems to be watching me as I put my phone in my coat pocket. I instinctively clutch the shopping bag emblazoned with a posh logo resting on my lap. Great—I just telegraphed that there's something valuable inside, when really all it contains are some old paperbacks Patty had given me at lunch to donate to the Little Free Library near my condo building.

The train arrives at my stop. I don't get up right away or make any move to leave. Instead I wait for the train doors to open and everyone standing nearby to exit. Just as the final announcement for my stop comes over the p.a. system, I quickly stand up and walk off the train...and so does mister baggy pants.

I don't like this. By giving everyone else a chance to get off first, I've fallen behind the departing group who are now descending the stairs to the street below, obstructing my only means of exit. I try to catch up without looking like I'm running scared. The hoodie hangs back, knowing there's nowhere for me to go. I can't tell if it's the same guy who followed me home from the train last time...he looks familiar. It's hard to know for sure with his loose clothes and the hoodie covering most of his face.

As I follow the group toward the bottom of the stairwell, I see over my shoulder that the hood has begun to descend the stairs. I could push past the people in front of me and make a run for it, but from his vantage at the top of the stairs he could watch where I go for blocks in either direction. Besides, I wore the only decent pair of non-gym shoes I own to comport with the dress code of the restaurant Patty chose for our long lunch, so I probably wouldn't be able to outrun him anyway.

The group disperses in all directions when we reach the street level. I make my way toward home, and once I turn the corner onto my darkened street I'm alone...until the hood rounds the same corner. He's succeeded at scaring me, which makes me angry. I guess this hood is going to get the Louisville Slugger treatment. I hope he's not the same guy as before and knows to expect it.

I arrive at my building and key in the security code. I push the door open and watch the hood through the glass. He stops when he spots me looking at him and then turns to walk in the other direction. Maybe the hood has cold feet... or a conscience. Either way, I'm pleased that my pleasant day won't have a messy ending.

I climb the stairs to my floor, ready to be home after what feels like a busy day, though I didn't really do much of anything. Once inside my condo unit, I lock the door behind me and flip the swing bar over the slide bolt. My first instinct is to pour myself a stiff drink and turn on the television, but I think better of it, deciding instead to make a pot of tea and try to get some writing done.

I drop my bag of books on the counter and take off my coat, tossing it onto the back of a chair. I pull the kettle down from its cupboard. As I'm filling it in the sink, I hear a knock at my door. That's strange...and disquieting. I return to the door and look through the peephole. The hood is standing on the other side, and all I can see is his mouth.

"Go away," I implore more than demand.

"I want to talk to you."

"Leave here...I warn you, I have a bat." Then I realize that I don't. Since my hands were occupied with a bag and keys, I forgot it in the doorjamb of the first unit.

"I'm not afraid of rabies."

"No...I have a baseball bat."

"Me too. I just found it at the top of the stairs."

"How did you get in here?" I ask.

"Same as you."

"I mean how did you get through the security door?" I clarify.

"I used the code: 4444. It's the only number on the keypad that doesn't feel stiff when you press it—not too smart."

"I didn't set up the code," I say defensively. Am I really having a conversation with this creep?

"Maybe you should ask management to change it."

"I'll do that," I say. "Now please go away, or I'll call the police."

"Just answer a question first."

"What is it?"

"Did you like my flowers?"

"That was you?" I ask.

"Yes, but I didn't know which unit was yours."

"Until you followed me up the stairs...waiting just long enough so that I wouldn't see you but that you could hear my door being locked. How did you know I was the only one who lived here?"

"You're the only person I've seen entering here after dark."

"And how did you know this was my floor and not the one above?"

"The hallway carpet on this floor is slightly worn."

"Okay, so why the dumb flowers and inept vandalism?"

"A peace offering."

"What does that mean?" I ask.

"A gift or gesture intended to end disputations and foster rapprochement. It comes from the Bible, though many mistakenly attribute it to Native Americans."

My mind figures out who is on the other side of the door before my brain can process it all. "I meant what does it mean in this context, Digy?"

"It means I'm sorry," Digy says as he pulls back his hood. "How did you know it was me?"

"A couple of the words you said didn't sound like simplEng."

"I was trying to put you off my scent…I guess my stratagem backfired." I can see through the peephole that his mouth is in the shape of a smile, but his eyes aren't squinting. "So how'd you figure it out?"

"Your mouth made a grimace when you used those words, as if you didn't approve of them," I answer. "So let me see if I've got this straight. You're here to say you're sorry…by scaring me half to death?"

"I didn't know you got scared."

"Everybody gets scared. I just don't fall to pieces about it. So what exactly are you apologizing for?"

"I'm not sure exactly, but when I saw you last it seemed as if my very existence somehow offended you. In fact I've always felt like you've had an aversion to me, and you're not a fatuous person who is easily offended, so I'm here to ask why."

"Oh Digy, get lost. You've never apologized for anything. You don't care what I think, and I've got better things to do than to help you feel better about your life by letting you take a tour through the mediocrity of mine. If you're upset about my column, then have your henchmen or hatchet men or whatever you call them do their worst. I've been kicked before, and I can get up again."

He doesn't say anything, but he doesn't move either. Is he surprised that I know why he's here like he was surprised a moment ago when I knew who he was? Or did he arrange for me to get a full-time column and is now taking a histrionic pause before reaching under the door to pull the rug from beneath my feet by telling me that I've been demoted to writing bumf for the horoscope section or some other such scut work.

"You just said one thing that is true and one that isn't," he tells me. "I don't recall having ever apologized for anything, and I had no intention of doing so now…at least not with any sincerity."

"So that's what I'm right about. What is it that you think I'm wrong about?" I ask, though I instantly regret it.

"You're wrong about me not valuing your opinion. I enjoy your writing; it surprises me. From sentence to sentence, I never know what you're going to write next…and that's a rare sensation for me. I envy that as a writer you can be anyone you want and express anything you wish."

"You're not going to tell me that you think I'm 'plugged in,' are you?"

"I don't know what that means, but let me prove my admiration by making a pair of unexpected requests that I expect will give me a turn to surprise you."

"Which are?" I ask.

"First, I'd like you to write my obituary."

"Is that a request or your way of informing me that you've wangled yourself into a position of authority at my paper and had me transferred to the obit section?"

"I have no authority over you and no interest in your newspaper," Digy answers. "I just want you to write something nice about me, and people typically write nice things in obituaries."

"But like you said before, my writing is surprising, so maybe I'll surprise everyone and write the cruelest obit ever."

"That might be fun too."

"Why are we talking about this?" I ask. "You're younger than I am. What makes you think I'll out live you? Besides, you're too important to die."

"I'm afraid that isn't true, and there are a great many people who believe the world would be better off if I were no longer on it."

"So you think somebody's going to murder you?"

"No, nothing like that. Anyway, I think such an action would be considered assassination or perhaps hericide in the old vernacular."

"More like ass-hole-cide. So then what...you got some kind of terminal illness?"

"Something like that. I think I might be suffering from the same terminal illness as your erstwhile roommate."

"You don't get to talk about him!" I wish the door was open so that I could slam it in his face.

"I didn't mean to upset you," he says pacifyingly. "Frankly, I didn't know you were capable of getting upset, but then there's a lot about you that I don't understand."

"Like what?" I ask, disappointed with myself for letting Digy get under my skin.

"You know, I did actually read all of your book. How did you know that your roommate was going to kill himself when he called you before you two were set to leave for spring break?"

"Digy...it was a long time ago."

"Yes, and I've only seen you once in the last twenty years, but it seems like you have me fairly well figured out, whereas you are an utter mystery to me."

"Have you ever been to a suicide's funeral?" I ask, touching the door.

"No, I've cared about so few people, and I have a strict rule about not attending ceremonies honoring people for whom I'm indifferent."

"If you had been to such a funeral, you wouldn't even think of taking your own life. You have a child who adores you, and you must know how Patty feels about you. Imagine the hurt you would cause them if they had to attend your selfish funeral."

"Since I was a science experiment pretty much from the age of two, I didn't really have a childhood, and so I never learned to live for others. I imagine I'm not unlike your roommate's father in that respect, but I see your point about those who care for me. When the time comes, I'll make sure it happens far away and there are ambiguities concerning the circumstances so that people can draw whatever conclusion they choose, though I had thought of requesting your assistance since you have some experience with such matters, but I suppose that's off the table now."

"It was never on the table, Digy. What I did all those years ago, I did to end the suffering of a good man and his son. You're not suffering, and you're not a good man."

"Again you've said one thing that is true and one that isn't, though this time I'll leave it for you to decide which is which."

Digy has now become an inopportune mystery to me—one that I need to understand. "If I'm to make an informed decision on that score, I'll need to ask you some questions."

"I don't promise to answer every question you ask, but I do promise to give a truthful response to every question I answer."

"My first question is: why?"

"I think you'd do well to remain a columnist," Digy says. "You'd have much to learn as an interviewer."

"You've put me in an awkward position, Digy."

"You think you're in an awkward position? I'm the one standing in an empty hallway talking to a door."

"I don't care about you at all, and so I don't care what happens to you…you know this about me."

"Yes, I think it's an honest way to live, though I imagine it's made for some lonely holidays."

"I do care about Patty and her son, so for them I will try to help you—"

"Do you mean help me down the stairs?"

"No," I answer, "help you the way I wish I could've helped my roommate."

"You still haven't told me how you knew he was going to take his own life when he called that night."

"His voice had changed…it sounded different. I'm not sure I can explain it."

"Does my voice now sound like his then?"

"I couldn't say, since I don't know you the way I knew him. I don't think anyone did."

"I certainly didn't know him well, but I could tell he was vivacious…so full of life. Ironic that he chose to empty himself of all that life at a young age, while you, who are practically the living dead, are still with us. If you knew him so well, why didn't you know the real reason he was in Study House?" Digy is trying to wound me with words, I assume just to see if he can. I won't give him the satisfaction twice. "Is it that you couldn't see his disorder, and so you didn't know him as well as you thought, or did you see it but decided to ignore it, and so you never truly accepted him for who he was?"

"I'm supposed to be the one asking the questions," I say.

"And as I recall, your concise question was 'why?' Why, when I have all the success and privilege anyone could hope for, would I want to end it? If you're smart, it makes you feel all the more ashamed when you're wrong."

"Only you could sound conceited about being humbled. So what were you wrong about?"

"I created simplEng to end the confusion caused by the complexity of our language in order to connect the disparate; now all those disparate people speak the same oversimplified language. They've learned the words I chose to the letter but they don't understand how to give them meaning. The writing they submit to my school, while technically proficient, is often incomprehensible because it's devoid of intention. I taught them the lyrics but not how to make the music."

"Is that why you have such a lugubrious outlook now?" I ask.

"No, I've always had a saturnine perspective owing to my intractable anhedonia, for it's in childhood that we develop our capacity for joy. I wanted to disrupt the education system that took my childhood from me to prove that I could, but now that it's broken I have no idea how to fix it. I never learned how to learn…I never had to, so what do I know about education? I've built this monstrous machine that I can't control and have no way of stopping."

"What about your new one-year bachelor's degree program?" I ask. "I mean it's not the most absurd thing I've ever heard. After all, I went to college for four years and hardly learned anything, so I figure somebody could just as easily learn almost nothing in one year."

"I shouldn't just be creating a different system, my métier should be to create a better system. The purpose of education is to give students a path to success. I changed the model for instruction, but I didn't make the path any clearer. The Flipped M School's early courses were brilliant. We recruited the best minds to share their knowledge and passion for their respective fields. It's a funny thing about fields though, people's understanding of them can be classified into four distinct groups, and I've discovered that the proportions of those groups are set in our nature, like the golden ratio in the natural world."

"Go on," I say, "but be warned, I was always dreadful at math."

"Then you would fall into the largest group for that particular field of study, who try as they might will never achieve any level of competence in the subject and will forever find it bewildering; these are the field's imbeciles. The second-largest group will achieve, with some effort, a partial understanding of the field and will revere those who more thoroughly comprehend it; these are the students. Those who are revered for their comprehensive understanding of the field and their ability to explain it so that it makes sense to the students are, of course, the teachers, but they are not the smallest group. The final and smallest group is comprised of the thought leaders, and they have more in common with the imbeciles than the students and teachers because for them the field isn't row upon row of neatly planted crops but rather an undomesticated wilderness whose chaos must be tamed by pioneers if it is ever to be cultivated."

"So what's your point?" I ask, not following any of this but not wanting Digy to explain it again either.

"These thought leaders were the subject matter experts and instructors for our early courses, and as as talented and inspired as they were, most of our students didn't understand their wild concepts. Our students, who mostly could only understand simplEng, needed simple concepts. Economics needed to be about money, not motives. History needed to be about dates, not ideas. So the thought leaders left, and we replaced them with new, so-called experts and instructors who taught the same old concepts in the same old ways."

"But even then," I say, trying to sound positive, which I'm sure instead sounds insincere, "you're offering free education to millions that's no worse than the typical education they'd get at colleges most of them couldn't afford anyhow."

"Which brings us to act two of this tragedy of errors. As more students signed up for our courses, the more courses we felt pressured to offer so that we could convince the cynics that our school was legitimate. We established degree programs before we found instructional designers to build courses for

them, and since we don't make our money from up-front tuition, and we can't get money from advertisers until there are
courses that are running for them to advertise in, we hired
designers who would work on the quick and instructors who
would teach on the cheap. Most of them were only nomi-
nally qualified—if that. Of course the ineluctable result was
courses far below the collegiate standard, of which I had always
thought so very little."

"But surely there must've been those inside the school that
saw what was happening," I say. "Why didn't anyone blow the
whistle?"

"Because we realized...no, I realized that if we were to
employ idiots to build and teach our courses, then we had to
hire even bigger idiots to supervise them. At the bottom of
this pitiful pyramid of higher education, we had underpaid
and overworked instructors who mostly shouldn't have been
teaching in the first place, but since they likely couldn't get jobs
teaching at other, more discerning institutions they were glad to
have the work, and so they passed students whose assignments
weren't up to par either because they were ill-equipped to assess
what par should've been or because they correctly understood
that if most of their students didn't pass they'd be out of work.
Above them were the subject matter experts and instructional
designers who built the courses. Their mandate was to build
courses fast, so there was no time for the experts to determine
the soundness of their program's objectives since their task was
only to create content for their assigned courses in the program,
not to review the courses that came before or after theirs in
the program's sequence, which were often built simultaneously
and thus usually imbricative and redundant. The designers, for
their part, had no time to verify the appropriateness of the content from the SMEs and no authority to question it since they
themselves typically didn't have a background in a given SME's

field. The department deans and program chairs—who were the biggest idiots and often minimally qualified themselves, believing that they had successfully faked it until they made it, and so kept their mouths shut when they didn't know something, which was frequently—were the ones who created the curricula and the ones who hired the instructors, SMEs, and designers. These middle managers were also charged with supervising everyone they hired, which required endless busywork that mostly involved attending pointless meetings and writing worthless reports about who knows what that were reviewed by who knows who. By hiring incompetent deans and chairs, we could be reasonably certain that they would be too overwhelmed to actually review the courses being built for their departments and programs and that, because they also happened to be overpaid, they would hire incompetent subordinates who would not jeopardize their jobs by questioning their dubious credentials or their ability to make decisions about fields with which they had at best only a cursory understanding. To further complicate the line of upward communication, we frequently shuffled middle management by cross-promoting them into different departments, which both made it seem as if the supervisors in charge of the instructors, SMEs, and designers were doing a good job and also made complaining to one's boss all the more impracticable since the complainers likely didn't know their bosses well and could be fairly sure they wouldn't be in the position long enough to accomplish any substantial change or cause any permanent damage.

"To further discourage internal condemnation, we let all those who built and taught the courses work remotely, since, after all, their students were remote, and we hired deans and chairs from different cities, so all these people actually had very limited contact with one another. I had in effect, half by accident and half on purpose, invented a flawlessly stupid system in which no one, except those of us at the very top, ever fully grasped their full measure of incompetence or complicity. There was no one to blow the whistle, because no one could completely comprehend the systemic defect at the center of it all. And, of course, this whole pyramid was putatively predicated on the goals of student achievement and advancement. Our students supported my system, and as it grew it crushed them."

"That sounds positively sinister," I say, aghast at the insidious machination of it all. "So why didn't your school implode early on?"

"Because it was propped up by expectation and expediency. For many of our students, this was their only exposure to formal education and their one opportunity to improve their station in life, so they trusted what we were teaching them, either because they didn't know better or because they weren't in a position to be discriminating. I doubt anyone thought they were getting the finest education, but the promise of free tuition proved meretricious enough. Students were passing courses and completing programs. We awarded degrees and created a new class of ostensibly educated workers in Third World countries across the globe. When we were accused by outsiders of building a Ponzi scheme, my rebuttal was that our detractors were simply outmoded elitists and that the entire education system is a Ponzi scheme free from entropy, for everyone is born uneducated, and so long as we continue to convince them that they need education, there will be a limitless supply of consumers."

"Seems like you had all the angles figured out." I put my back against the door and slide down to the floor.

"That's the downside of having a vision, you can convince yourself that your plans are viable and your intentions tenable almost as easily as you convince others. After all those years I spent studying the dictionary, I learned that language is neither right nor wrong. It's a tool, akin to dynamite, that can be used for both good and bad. With it we can shape mountains into monuments, articulating our aspirations. Or we can use it to destroy the things that others have built, senselessly codifying the bits of rubble that remain after the explosion. Do you know what I'm trying to say?"

"I think your metaphor was slightly catachrestic," I criticize, "but yes…I'm following you."

"Knowing that what you study can create either purpose or meaninglessness comes at a cost that is dear. In the time I spent examining our language, I discovered the futility of learning. I made it my goal to use my gifts to recast the education system, and instead the only gift I shared was the futility I had found. All those years were wasted, and then I went on to waste the time of legions the world over who in aggregate lost almost incalculable years studying through my farce of a school. The abbreviated bachelor's program we announced yesterday was my last, best effort to minimize the damage my school was doing, since at least our students would only lose a single year earning a degree, but my plan to bow out gracefully by disassociating myself from the school and turning it over to new leadership while it's still on an upward trajectory has been thwarted. I was aware that the school's scudding ascendency had been drawing increased scrutiny to our operations; however, I was caught completely unawares by the revelation that a fraud case is being amassed against my school and me personally, which will be heard by an international tribunal. The prospect of being humiliated on such a prominent stage is more than my ego can bear."

I hear him put his back to the door and take a seat on the floor as I have. I don't know what to say, but I know I need to say something. "So you made a mistake…what's the worst that could happen?"

"I've made enemies of many powerful people over the years, so I anticipate that my very public pillorying will make the Nuremberg Trials seem like a Friars' Roast."

"Okay, so make your public apology, try to make amends, and then move on."

"I never had a backup plan. This school was my life's work. I did the best I could, and I was found lacking…and ultimately my efforts will be proven nocent."

"Then your work is done," I say. "Retire in luxury. Use your money to live the childhood you never had."

"That's the thing with time—not just the minutes and hours, but the times in our lives—once they're gone they never return. As for my money, I intend to use half of it in an attempt to repay all the students who ever took a Flipped M course, which works out to about nine dollars for each of them."

"And the other half?" I ask.

"I'm leaving it to my children."

"I thought the son you had with Patty was your only child."

"That brings me to my second request."

"I haven't agreed to the first one yet…wait—what?" I stand and look through the peephole. Digy must've stood up at the same time, because I see him trying to look through the other end. His eyeball is so magnified that I have an optometrist's view of the blood vessels in the whites of his eye.

"Are you surprised?" he asks. "I can't tell. Ironically, I don't think I've ever been in such close proximity to you, but through this peephole you look shapeless and faraway."

"I'm right here, and I'm more confused than surprised," I say. "So what's your second request exactly?"

"For you to be the mother of my second child, of course."

"How can you even ask me that? You just told me you want to end your life and now you're telling me you want to create a new one."

"It makes perfect sense, if you think about it."

"If by perfect sense you mean zero sense, then you might be right."

"Nothing is perfect, and zero is nothing," he says glibly, "so sure that works too."

"Digy, stop being you for a moment and answer my next question: why?"

"What your question lacks in originality it makes up for in succinctness. Let's start with you. You want a child. I've seen how you are with my son; around him you're a completely different person—one with feelings."

"I can't be a mother. I'm like three people rolled into one, and yet somehow there are still parts of me that are missing."

"And a child would help you fill in those lacunae."

"Have you been attempting to cozen me with your non-simplEng vocabulary?" I ask.

"I would never resort to such blandishments. I honestly think you'd make a terrific mother. As far as I know, you've only loved one person in your whole life, and in an effort to secure his happiness, you did something that no one else ever would. There is no sacrifice you would not make for your child, and I can tell you from personal experience that they imbue life with a purpose you never thought possible. Children are vivifying."

"And yet you want to kill yourself."

"It seems we're on to me now. I love my son more than anything, but I know he'd be better off without me in his life. I can't help but try to control everything around me—it's part of my character caused by an intrinsic and ineludible disorder— and I've come to understand that although my aim is always for betterment, the outcomes are often disastrous. By the time my son was born, my apostasy from language was absolute, so I thought it would be better for him if he weren't exposed to it, learning instead to read body language, which is a manifestly more honest form of communication."

"Now you think otherwise?" I ask.

"I never told Patty this, but I had a team of geneticists examine her family's medical history and test a sample of her DNA. They concluded that there was a moderate probability that she would pass down her personality transitioning. I thought that by sheltering our son from the outside world, we could mitigate that risk, but for some time now I've seen him transitioning through the changing ways he looks at me. By keeping language and the world from my son, all I've managed to do is exacerbate his condition. My son will be afforded every opportunity, but even so I fear he'll never make his mark on the world. And so I want to leave behind another child who I hope can undo what I have done—a child who I have no influence over and who isn't affected by every little thing. Think of the potential for a child who had the best parts of both of us. I would be proud for that to be my legacy."

"Patty would be so angry with—"

"So don't tell her," Digy says simply. "She doesn't need to know I'm the father. You wouldn't even have to tell our child for that matter."

"That wouldn't bother you?"

"It would if I were going to be around."

"I understand your logic," I say, "but I don't know how I can make this decision."

"What if you don't have to? What if I tell you my second request isn't actually that we make a child together but rather that you keep the child already growing inside of you?"

"What the hell are you talking about?"

"Your new gynecologist," Digy answers, "I paid off her student loans from medical school, freeing her from having to stay in her lucrative but lackluster job here in the states so that she can pursue her dream of opening a women's health clinic in some African country. I forget which, but I'm paying for that too."

"Why would you do that?"

"So that she would inseminate you with my sperm during your exam. I imagine you must've thought the exam quite different from the last one you had all those years ago."

I pound the door with my fists and then kick it hard. "You son of a bitch—I won't give you the chance to commit suicide."

"Calm down," Digy says in a soothing voice. "I was only cutting a dido."

"Damn you…it wasn't funny." I use the back of my hands to wipe hot tears from my face.

"Are you sure? I had to swallow a laugh from deep in my belly."

"Mine must've been down so deep that it couldn't find its way out," I say, trying to regain my composure. "So then you didn't really pay off my doctor's loans and agree to fund a clinic?"

"I did do that, but only for her to check if you're, uh… fertile. Still highly unethical, of course, but she was alright with it considering the good she can accomplish overseas. Anyway, I'm pleased to inform you that you are…right now in fact, but obviously the choice is yours—though let me ask you, for that moment when you thought you'd been impregnated, was your first instinct to keep the baby?"

"My first instinct was to put your head on a pike."

"So no initial thoughts about the baby you believed you might be carrying?" Digy asks.

"I saw myself holding a baby in prison," I say as I release a deep breath I'd been holding for what feels like forever.

"You really were thinking of killing me. Maybe it wasn't such an amusing dido after all. One last question then: I've been standing in you doorway for nearly an eternity. Will you let me in?"

Chapter Sixteen

Ringing that causes wringing. Specifically, the ringing of church bells seems to wring the hearts of the few who have gathered for Digy's graveside funeral service...though not mine. I feel for Patty, so I'm here to support her, but it was all I could do to write Digy's obituary as he requested, and if I hadn't been desperate for a column topic the day his death was reported I might not have done it.

Peter and I stand behind the last row of wooden folding chairs, which have been arranged into a tidy rectangle on a thin, green carpet that looks as if it was ordered from a miniature golf catalog. Despite the summer sun and my very pregnant condition, I demur when Peter suggests that I have a seat. There don't seem to be enough chairs for all the people that I imagine would attend the funeral for a person of Digy's stature.

"I'd feel like a terrible person for taking the chair of an elderly mourner who knew Digy well," I say.

"You mean you feel like a terrible person, because you don't feel terrible that he's dead," Peter says.

"Wow," I say sarcastically, "your powers of perception are staggering."

"Judging by the paucity of attendees, I don't think you're the only one who's not broken up about his passing." He ignored my derisory sarcasm. He's been doing that a lot lately, and I adore him for it.

"There must've been a private ceremony before this one for those who were closest to him," I hypothesize. "I'm sure they'll be arriving soon."

"Well, it's a funeral, so it's not as if there's assigned seating." He still doesn't seem accustomed to standing in direct sunlight, despite having been out of prison for several months now. "Besides, they'd have to be pretty late, as we're a little late ourselves and hardly anyone is here."

"Yes, but you know how reluctant people are to accept a seat offered by a pregnant lady. I'd be miserable if the seats suddenly filled up with bereaved latecomers, and I was stuck sitting near a standing octogenarian."

"But you look miserable now in this heat," he protests.

"Then I'm fated to be miserable either way, so what's the difference?"

"Let's take these two seats on the end of this last row. If a swarm of geriatric grievers abruptly arrives, it's not like they're going to sprint over here from their cars, so we'll have plenty of time to stand up and ensure that there is adequate seating for the senescent—problem solved."

"We'll see," I say as I sit in the row's penultimate chair.

"The plan will work," he assures me with a smile, "I'm certain of it."

"I find your certainty as irritating as your considerateness."

"Oh, you're pregnant…everything makes you irritable."

We turn to see a lone limousine pull up with a few sedans following slowly behind. The chauffer gets out and opens the passenger door near the curb. Patty is the first to exit. I've never seen her wear black before. She looks so small behind her oversized sunglasses. She reaches inside to help her son out of the backseat. He's grown so much since the last time I saw him.

"So that's Patty's boy?" Peter asks rhetorically. "He's a cute kid."

"He's got a cute mother, but I wasn't sure if she would bring him."

I wave at Patty and her son as they approach. His eyes light up with recognition, but Patty is stone-faced. She looks as if she might walk past without acknowledging us, but then she stops at our row. We stand, and I move to give her a hug.

"You don't have to do that," Patty says curtly. "I know how much you abhor physical contact."

"Is it okay?" I ask in a soft voice.

"What, to talk in front of my son? Yes, the first words he heard were me telling him that his father was dead. His vocabulary has been growing at an astounding rate ever since. He's even chosen a name for himself."

"What's your name little man?" asks Peter.

The little boy looks down at the ground, thinks for a moment, and then moves to hide behind his mother.

"As you might imagine," Patty says, "he's a little shy around new people—especially convicted felons."

"Patty," I say firmly, "Peter and I are together now."

"Isn't that lovely for the two of you. And you thought to bring the Psycho to Digy's funeral. It's like the class reunion we never had."

"Patty, I know you're hurting, but—" I begin to say as Peter gently grabs my arm.

"Yes, it's been a difficult week," Patty says, as she tilts her head and dabs under her sunglasses with a handkerchief. "But that's no reason for me to be rude…I'm sorry. Thank you both for coming."

"No problem," Peter replies.

"You're looking fit these days," Patty compliments, putting her handkerchief back in her purse and snapping it shut.

"Well the prison had a gym, and I had plenty of free time."

"To answer your earlier question," Patty says, ignoring Peter's attempt to inject a little humor into our colloquy, "my son has chosen to take my name for his first name and his father's for his last."

"His name is Patricia?" I ask without taking a moment to think it through.

"Of course not," Patty answers, "he's using my surname, Bell, for his first name. Granted, it's a bit unorthodox, but I'm sure he'll make it his own as he grows into it."

"It's not so unusual," says Peter. "Bell...short for Welliam. It's a pleasure to meet you Bell."

"Patty," I say, "I've tried to call you about a dozen times this week...I've been trying to get in touch with you for months."

"I know," Patty says. "I apologize again. Even before Digy's passing, life had been...trying."

"If there's anything I can do to help—"

"Yes, Vivien, I'll be sure to let you know. But for now, the show must go on. Feel free to move closer to the front, though I can't promise the performance will be entertaining, and as you can see there won't be much of an audience."

With that, Patty takes Bell in hand, and they move to take a seat in the middle of the front row. A few other people milling around follow her lead and sit down. Only the first couple of rows are full, with the rows behind intermittently filled in, leaving me and Peter as the only occupants of the last row.

Patty cues the hovering minister with a nod, and he takes his place in front of the closed casket.

"Welcome," he says in a voice that is somehow both somber and buoyant. "Today is a hard day for us all. Both for you as friends and family who have lost a loved one and for me as a minister who has been tasked with saying charitable things about a man I only knew from the news, which has been less than charitable toward him of late."

I hear a few chuckles. The minister's candor seems to have lightened the weight over this service.

"Usually in these situations when I did not know the deceased personally, I open with a few agnostic bromides, read a couple of comforting verses from the Good Book, and close with an ecumenical homily. However, as I understand it, Mr. Wether, or 'Digy' as he was affectionately known to many of you, was not a spiritual man. And, as it sometimes happens, his last will and testament was very specific about his wishes for his eulogy. Particularly that the minister not prattle on endlessly."

I hear more chuckling. A woman two rows in front of me shakes her head, and I can tell by the corners of her mouth that she is grinning.

"I can't say I blame him for that," the minister adds with a wry smile. "No one wants to hear a lot of hot air on a warm day."

The laughter is louder now. I notice a slight breeze and the heat doesn't feel so oppressive anymore.

"But let me leave you with one final thought. I know there have been conflicting accounts circulating about the circumstances of Mr. Wether's demise, and certainly there has been rampant speculation surrounding the events of his final days. As I'm sure you're all aware, the coffin behind me is empty, but let it not be a hollow symbol. It's a cliché to ask that you not dwell on a man's death, but rather think of his life. And still, even that proposition is fraught with difficulties, given the many sordid allegations that have recently come to light regarding Mr. Wether's business practices. However, we are here today both to pay our final respects to this man and to bury the past. So I ask that you also bury any misgivings you may harbor about his character. Remember not his squandered potential that resulted in ruin as he neared the great compromise that is middle age, but instead of the promise he showed as a young man. That's what I encourage you to take from here today: your wonder at the promise that once was, for it still exists in our world today."

The woman in front of me who had been shaking her head in mirth now nods her head in agreement.

"Now I'll ask Ms. Bell, a woman who knew Mr. Wether well, to come up and say a few words."

The minister takes two steps backwards as Patty rises and takes position in front of the casket.

"I'm not sure anyone knew Digy well," Patty begins, "but I suppose I knew him better than most; however, per his specific wishes that the minster previously mentioned, the words I say will not be my own but rather those from an obituary of sorts written by a local newspaper columnist."

Patty pulls a folded newspaper clipping from her purse. Peter looks at me as if to ask, *Did you know about this?* I shrug and give him a nonplussed expression. Patty unfolds my column and begins reading aloud.

"'I have never been able to read people…I don't even really know what that means. In college, with a friend's help, this is how I finally learned to make sense of the things people do: Every action has multiple possible motives. Since I lack the innate ability to accurately ascribe a particular motive to a given action, I must consider all the potential motives of many actions and then look for patterns.

"'A man steals. The motive for the theft might be a simple thrill or a desperate need—maybe you can judge why the thief stole by looking at him or listening to him speak, but I cannot. So I go on to assess the possible motives of his next action and then the next, always searching for a pattern. Ironically, I have found—over time, as the sample size grows—that I become a better judge of character than most for the same reason I wasn't a good judge of character in the first place, because I don't judge people by how they seem, but rather by what they do.

"'This is how I taught myself to understand people, and it worked…on almost everyone. Today someone I knew died. You knew him too. I'm sure you were informed of his death via every Internet connected device in your possession moments after it was discovered. I've known Digy, as we used to call him, since college when I first developed my process. I did not know him well then, and we did not keep in contact afterwards. Since that time, I only knew of him what I saw or read in the news. However, over the years he's been in the news plenty, offering a substantial sample size, and yet I still don't know what to make of him.

"'I never thought of him as an especially good man, but I knew him to be a complex man of redoubtable keenness and worthy of consideration. He wasn't the sort of person best suited to be a leader as he might've believed himself to be, but nevertheless I thought of him as a cynosure whom we could learn from. With all the ingenuous, easily-understood people in the world—even by me—perhaps we should reckon the ingenious and insoluble somewhat differently.

"'There are only so many fundamental forces in our human nature, but they manifest themselves in a nearly infinite number of ways; however, if you understand the forces themselves, the actions they impel have their own discernable logic and even become predictable. I won't tell you that Digy was a force of nature, but I do think that his illimitably ambitious nature came from an elemental desire to improve our condition. He believed that the state of the world was wanting, and he thought he could fix it. That might smack of hubris, but it should also sound like caring.

"'I know there will be much ado over how Digy died. I've seen this situation too many times before. The news is the loudest when it has the least to report. However, I'm choosing to turn down the volume and arrive at my own conclusions. Digy did not believe himself to be an ordinary machine made of bone and flesh, but rather an inimitable entity with agency and purpose. You could see it in the choices he made. Even all those years ago, I knew that he would live life on his own terms and never quit until he had exploited his gifts to the fullest—a sound strategy for us all.

"'I want to share with you something he once told me. It made me so angry that I still remember it clearly. He opposed the building of a costly community outreach library on campus in favor of a far cheaper plan to add a few benches and some shade trees to the empty lot on which the library was to be built. He said: People don't want to read. In their busy, noisy lives they want the calm, quiet environment in which reading is done. They're not looking for literature; they're looking for a respite. They won't come for books; they'll come for the chance to contemplate.

"'Perhaps eventually, when the noise dies down, the salutary effect of Digy's absence will be a few more quiet moments for us all to contemplate. I modestly suggest that we spend some of that time contemplating his life and how he influenced ours. His legacy won't be measured in libraries, but maybe he was right when he told me that's not what we really want. After a lifetime spent in the sun, I hope he found his peaceful place in the shade. He deserves no more and no less—just like the rest of us.'"

Patty statuesquely holds the clipping in her hand for a moment, and then lets it fall as her hand drops to her side. The breeze catches it, blowing it over the casket, fluttering from sight—perhaps into the six-foot hole beyond or maybe farther. She looks as if she might say something more, but instead she retakes her seat next to her son.

The minister gestures that we are free to leave and thanks us for coming. Patty remains seated as a few people around her offer their condolences. Peter and I wait our turn as those nearest to her disperse. The wind has picked up, as if exhorting the funeralgoers to be on their way so that the work of putting the vacant coffin in the ground can begin.

Patty and Bell rise to leave only after all but a few mourners have returned to their cars and driven off. We stand and wait for them beside the last row of chairs as they walk toward their limousine. Again, with her dark sunglasses on, Patty looks as if she does not see me.

"Patty," I say to get her attention, though she is only feet from me, and we're nearly the only ones left.

"Yes," she says, stopping in front of me.

"I'm so sorry," I say, though I'm unsure for what specifically. "If I had known Digy would request that my column be read here, I would've written it differently."

"It was fine," she tells me. "I thought you wrote some kind things."

"But if there was anything…that you didn't think was kind then I—"

"Everything you wrote was true, and Digy would have appreciated that," Patty says. "On several occasions, I heard him praise your authentic writing aesthetic."

"I didn't realize he liked my work."

A tree blowing in the wind casts a moving shadow over Patty's face. I can see the clouds rolling in reflected on the opaque lenses of her glasses.

"I think you did," Patty calmly accuses. "But the me that I am now has nothing further to say about esthetics…or anything else for that matter."

I drop my head and once more offer a feeble, "I'm sorry."

"Yes, you've said that already…we all have," Patty says. "Now it's time for us to move on."

"I don't know…are you sure?" I ask.

"I've never been more certain of anything."

About the Author

Wes Payton has a B.A. in Rhetoric/Philosophy and an M.A. in English, having written a play for his master's thesis. His play *Way Station* was selected for a Next Draft reading in 2015, and *What Does a Question Weigh?* was selected for a staged reading as part of the 2017 Chicago New Work Festival. His first novel, *Lead Tears*, was released in 2016, and his second novel, *Darkling Spinster*, was published in 2017 by an imprint of Start Media. He has also been a short-story presenter for the Illinois Philological Association. *Standing in Doorways* is his third novel.